OPEN

New York City, Summer/Fall 2004
Number Nineteen

 # OPEN CITY

Actual Air
Poems by David Berman

"David Berman's poems are beautiful, strange, intelligent, and funny. They are narratives that freeze life in impossible contortions. They take the familiar and make it new, so new the reader is stunned and will not soon forget. I found much to savor on every page of *Actual Air*. It's a book for everyone."
— James Tate

"This is the voice I have been waiting so long to hear . . . Any reader who tunes in to his snappy, offbeat meditations is in for a steady infusion of surprises and delights."
— Billy Collins

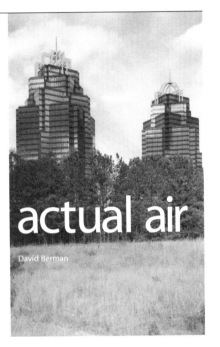

My Misspent Youth
Essays by Meghan Daum

"An empathic reporter and a provocative autobiographer . . . I finished it in a single afternoon, mesmerized and sputtering."
— *The Nation*

"Meghan Daum articulates the only secret left in the culture: discreet but powerful fantasies of romance, elegance, and ease that survive in our uncomfortable world of striving. These essays are very smart and very witty and just heartbreaking enough to be deeply pleasurable."
— Marcelle Clements

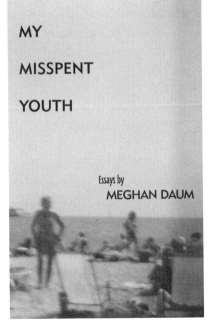

BOOKS

Venus Drive
Stories by Sam Lipsyte

"I like it when short stories—metaphorically speaking, of course, smack me in the face, kind of llike what Kafka said about art being like an axe. And so that's what Sam Lipsyte's stories do— they come at you like a fist, they knock you around, they make you wince, they make you look away, and then they make you look back."
   —Jonathan Ames

"It's a dark thrill to tap into the sensibility of Sam Lipsyte's remarkable stories. *Venus Drive* is a dazzling debut."
   —Robert Olen Butler

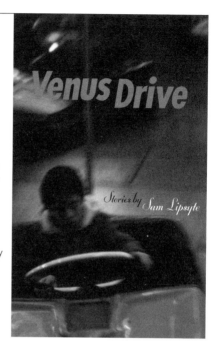

World on Fire
by Michael Brownstein

"Bold and ambitious, *World on Fire* engages the great issues of the day, mixing the personal with the political, demanding attention be paid, continuing in the great tradition of Whitman, Ginsberg, and Pound. Here's a howl for the twenty-first century."
   —Eric Schlosser, author of
      Fast Food Nation

"One of the most eloquent recent poetic works to cover the downsides of 'progress' and to cry out for a counterpunch against the manipulations of empire."
   —*Publishers Weekly* (starred review)

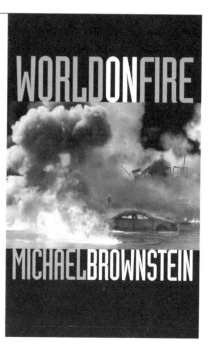

OPEN CITY

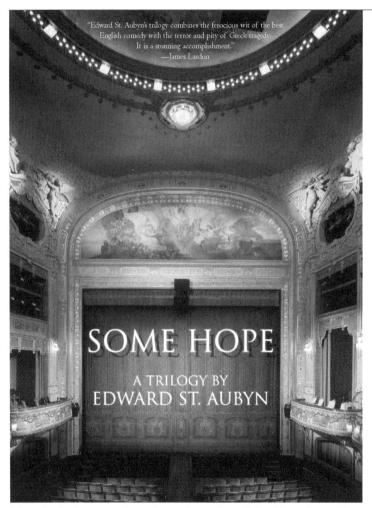

"Edward St. Aubyn's trilogy combines the ferocious wit of the best English comedy with the terror and pity of Greek tragedy. It is a stunning accomplishment."
—James Lasdun

SOME HOPE

A TRILOGY BY
EDWARD ST. AUBYN

"Speedballs, incest, and royalty are just a few of the things that make *Some Hope* exquisitely harrowing entertainment. Beyond the high-born squalor, though, is a saga of genuine wit and heartache."
—Sam Lipsyte

"A masterpiece. Edward St. Aubyn is a writer of immense gifts. His wit, his profound intelligence, and his exquisite control of a story that rapidly descends to the lower depths before somehow painfully rising again—all go to distinguish the trilogy as fiction of a truly rare and extraordinary quality."
—Patrick McGrath

A Barnes & Noble Discover Great New Writers selection

BOOKS

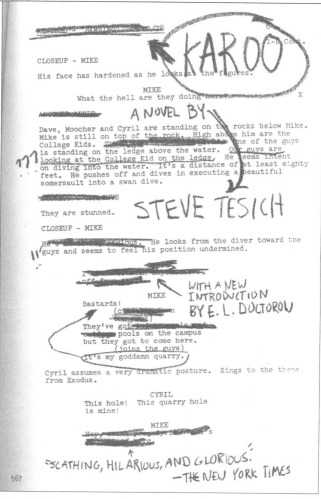

CLOSEUP - MIKE

His face has hardened as he looks at the figures.

MIKE
What the hell are they doing here?

Dave, Moocher and Cyril are standing on the rocks below Mike. Mike is still on top of the rock. High above him are the College Kids. One of the guys is standing on the ledge above the water. Our guys are looking at the College Kid on the ledge. He seems intent on diving into the water. It's a distance of at least eighty feet. He pushes off and dives in executing a beautiful somersault into a swan dive.

They are stunned.

CLOSEUP - MIKE

He looks from the diver toward the guys and seems to feel his position undermined.

MIKE
Bastards!
They've got pools on the campus but they got to come here.
(joins the guys)
It's my goddamn quarry.

Cyril assumes a very dramatic posture. Sings to the theme from Exodus.

CYRIL
This hole! This quarry hole is mine!

MIKE

567

KAROO

A NOVEL BY

STEVE TESICH

WITH A NEW INTRODUCTION BY E. L. DOCTOROW

"SCATHING, HILARIOUS, AND GLORIOUS."
—THE NEW YORK TIMES

"Fascinating—a real satiric invention full of wise outrage."
—Arthur Miller

"A powerful and deeply disturbing portrait of a flawed, self-destructive, and compulsively fascinating figure."
—*Kirkus Reviews* (starred)

"Saul Karoo is a new kind of wild man, the sane maniac. Larger than life and all too human, his out-of-control odyssey through sex, death, and show business is extreme, and so is the pleasure of reading it. Steve Tesich created a fabulously Gargantuan comic character."
—Michael Herr

Ice chunk falls from sky onto car dealership

Whack named top dispatcher

Soccer tea...

AT A GLANCE

Associated Press

Madagascan soccer authorities plan to take severe action against club Stade Olympique l'Emyrne, who scored 149 own-goals in protest against alleged refereeing bias in a match on Thursday.

SOE lost, 149-0, to AS Adema in the last game of the Indian Ocean island's league championship. SOE's coach Ratsimandresy Ratsarazaka orchestrated the protest from the stands as the team began repeatedly firing shots into its own net from the opening whistle.

RUNNING

The Minus Times

EVERYWHERE AND NOWHERE
SINCE 1992

A SOUTHERN LITERARY ALMANAC

WWW.MINUSTIMES.COM

OPEN CITY

a girl could stand up

[A NOVEL]

LESLIE MARSHALL

Grove Press

An imprint of Grove/Atlantic, Inc.
Distributed by Publishers Group West

PEN American Center announces the recipients of the

2004 PEN/ROBERT BINGHAM FELLOWSHIPS FOR WRITERS

JONATHAN SAFRAN FOER
Author of *Everything is Illuminated*

WILL HEINRICH
Author of *The King's Evil*

MONIQUE TRUONG
Author of *The Book of Salt*

The biennial PEN/Robert Bingham Fellowship honors exceptionally talented fiction writers whose debut work was published in the previous two years. Bingham Fellows undertake and complete a project of public literary service under the auspices of PEN. For more information, visit **www.pen.org**

OPEN CITY

Open City is published triannually by Open City, Inc., a not-for-profit corporation. Donations are tax-deductible to the extent allowed by the law. A one-year subscription (3 issues) is $30; a two-year subscription (6 issues) is $55. Make checks payable to: Open City, Inc., 270 Lafayette Street, Suite 1412, New York, NY 10012. For credit-card orders, see our Web site: www.opencity.org. E-mail: editors@opencity.org.

Open City is a member of the Council of Literary Magazines and Presses and is indexed by the American Humanities Index.

Front and back cover by Wayne Gonzales. Front: *The Carousel Club,* 2002; 74 x 60 inches; acrylic on canvas; private collection; courtesy Paula Cooper Gallery, New York. Back: *Self-Portrait as a Young Marine,* 2004; 52 x 41 inches; acrylic on canvas; courtesy Paula Cooper Gallery, New York, and Galerie Almine Rech, Paris.

Front page painting by Sally Ross, 1999; 50 x 40 inches; oil on linen.

Open City gratefully acknowledges the generous support of the family of Robert Bingham. We also thank the Greenwall Foundation and the New York State Council on the Arts.

State of the Arts

NYSCA

The editors would like to congratulate Craig Arnold for the selection of his poem, "Your friend's arriving on the bus" (from *Open City* #16) for *Best American Poetry* 2004.

OPEN CITY

EDITORS
Thomas Beller
Joanna Yas

ART DIRECTOR
Nick Stone

EDITORS-AT-LARGE
Adrian Dannatt
Elizabeth Schmidt

ASSISTANT EDITOR
Alicia Bergman

CONTRIBUTING EDITORS
David Berman
Aimée Bianca
Will Blythe
Lee Ann Brown
Sam Brumbaugh
Vanessa Chase
Amanda Gersh
Laura Hoffmann
Kip Kotzen
Anthony Lacavaro
Alix Lambert
Sam Lipsyte
Jim Merlis
Honor Moore
Parker Posey
Alexandra Tager
Tony Torn
Lee Smith
Jocko Weyland

INTERNS
Carla Blumenkranz
Simone Gorrindo

READERS
Gabriel Marc Delahaye
Leah Greenstein
Jessica Hoffmann
Allison Lorentzen
Nadxieli Mannello

FOUNDING EDITORS
Thomas Beller
Daniel Pinchbeck

FOUNDING PUBLISHER
Robert Bingham

LINCOLN PLAZA CINEMAS

Six Screens

63RD STREET & BROADWAY
OPPOSITE LINCOLN CENTER
212-757-2280

NEW LITERARY AWARD!

FIRST ANNUAL
RROFIHE TROPHY

FOR AN UNPUBLISHED SHORT STORY
(UP TO 5,000 WORDS)

WINNER RECEIVES:
$500 CASH
TROPHY
PUBLICATION IN OPEN CITY

JUDGED BY RICK ROFIHE

GUIDELINES

☞ Stories should be typed, double-spaced, on 8 1/2 x 11 paper with the author's name and contact information on the first page and name and story title on the upper right corner of remaining pages.

☞ Submissions must be postmarked by September 15, 2004

☞ Limit one submission per author

☞ Author must not have been previously published in *Open City*

☞ Mail submissions to RRofihe, 341 Lafayette Street, #974, New York, NY 10012

☞ Enclose self-addressed stamped business envelope to receive names of winner and honorable mentions

☞ All manuscripts are non-returnable and will be recycled.

☞ Reading fee is $10. Check or money order payable to RRofihe

Rick Rofihe is the author of *Father Must*, a collection of short stories published by Farrar, Straus & Giroux. His fiction has appeared in *The New Yorker*, *Grand Street*, *Open City*, and on epiphanyzine.com. His nonfiction has appeared in *The New York Times*, *The Village Voice*, Spy, and *The East Hampton Star*, and on mrbellersneighborhood.com. A recipient of the Whiting Writers' Award, he has taught writing at Columbia University and the Writer's Voice of the West Side Y. He currently teaches privately and at Gotham Writers' Workshop in New York.

GRANTA

WE CONFESS: We're So Confident That You'll Love GRANTA That We're Willing To Give It To You—FREE!

FREE WITH THIS OFFER

As a reader of these pages, we believe that you subscribe to the view that good writing matters. And *Granta* exists to publish it.

Since 1979, *Granta* has published some of the world's finest writers, tackling the world's most important subjects, from intimate human experiences to the large public and political events that shape all of our lives. Each issue features a rich diversity of stories—the best new fiction, memoir, reportage, travel, essays (and photography) that *Granta* can commission, inspire or find.

PLUS: With this introductory offer, we'll send you our brand new anthology, *A Granta Confessional*, featuring seven classic *Granta* pieces never collected in book form before and not available anywhere else, including:

KATHRYN CHETKOVICH on envying the success of the famous writer she lives with; **ARIEL DORFMAN** on feeling a pang of indifference at the sight of a drowning America boy; **GEOFF DYER** on his hallucinogenic search for oblivion; **JAMES HAMILTON-PATERSON** on being raped and wondering whether he might have asked for it; **BLAKE MORRISON** on letting anger get the best of him when his son's bicycle is stolen; **GEORGES PEREC** on creating an inventory of all he's eaten (and drunk) in the course of a year; and **EDMUND WHITE** on leaving behind the talking cure.

In all you get:

➤ *A Granta Confessional*—a 128-page paperback book FREE.

➤ **A DEEPLY DISCOUNTED OFFER:** A year's subscription to *Granta* magazine (four quarterly paperback issues of at least 256 pages each worth $14.95 each) for just $24.95.

➤ **A MONEY-BACK GUARANTEE.** You may cancel your subscription at any time, for any reason, and we immediately will refund your payment for all remaining unmailed issues. *A Granta Confessional* is free, regardless of whether you continue to subscribe or not.

➤ That's $59.80 worth of reading—plus a free book—for just $24.95. Altogether, you save $34.85 (58%) with this offer.

CONTRIBUTORS' NOTES

BILL ADAMS is an artist who lives in New York. He recently showed his paintings and drawings at K.S. Art in New York.

JACK ANDERSON is the author of nine books of prose poems and line-and-stanza poems. His poems have appeared in many literary magazines and anthologies and one of his prose poems provided the title for the New Rivers Press anthology *The Party Train* (1996). He is also a dance historian and a critic for *The New York Times* and *The Dancing Times* of London and coeditor (with George Dorris) of *Dance Chronicle,* a journal of dance history.

PRISCILLA BECKER writes poetry, essays, and criticism. She runs a poetry workshop in the Boerum Hill section of Brooklyn and is the author of a book of poems, *Internal West.* The editors apologize for an error in *Open City* #18 whereby her byline and title ("Blue Statuary") sat atop William Wenthe's poem (which is actually called "Against Witness"). Priscilla's correct poem appears in this issue (along with a new one).

JOSHUA BECKMAN is the author of four books of poetry, most recently *Your Time Has Come* (Verse Press, 2004). A CD, *Adventures While Preaching the Gospel of Beauty*, featuring his collaborative poetry with Matthew Rohrer, was released in 2004. He lives in Staten Island.

JASON BROWN has published one collection, *Driving the Heart and Other Stories* (W.W. Norton). "North" is from a new collection all about the same town called *The Town by the River.* He teaches in the MFA program at the University of Arizona.

ROBERT OLEN BUTLER has published ten novels and three volumes of short stories, one of which, *A Good Scent from a Strange Mountain*, won the 1993 Pulitzer Prize for Fiction. His new book of stories, *Had a Good Time*, was inspired by his collection of antique picture postcards. The assembled heads of Severance will first appear next spring in French (Rivages) to coincide with a ballet based upon them which will be performed in Lyons. A recipient of a Guggenheim Fellowship in fiction, he also won a National Magazine Award for Fiction. He teaches in the creative writing program at Florida State University.

BRYAN CHARLES grew up in Michigan.

Born in 1920, **TREVOR DANNATT** has published widely, including nine editions of the *Architects' Yearbook* (1945–60), *Modern Architecture in Britain* (1959), *Architecture, Education, and Research: The Work of Leslie Martin* (1996), *Trevor Dannatt: Buildings and Interiors, 1951–1972*, a monograph. An academician at London's Royal Academy and honorary member of the American Institute of Architects, he has maintained his own architectural practice for over fifty years. Built works include the Friends' Meeting House, Blackheath, London;

the Victoria Gate Entrance and Visitor Centre at the Royal Botanic Gardens, Kew; Vaughan College, Leicester; the King Faisal Conference Centre, Mosque, and Hotel in Riyadh; and the British Embassy in that same city. These are his first published poems.

AMBER DERMONT is the fiction writer-in-residence at Rice University in Houston. Her work received Special Mention in the 2004 *Pushcart Prize* anthology, and has recently appeared in *Alaska Quarterly Review, The Gettysburg Review, Seneca Review,* and *Zoetrope.*

NORMAN DOUGLAS has played many roles; some good, some he'd rather not recall. Although the past is gone, "Male Order," was written in 1985 for Tina—who was last heard from in Guadalajara—and her nephew. Thanks for being there.

JULIANA ELLMAN lives and works in Brooklyn. She has shown her work with Marc Foxx in Los Angeles and Lombard-Freid Fine Arts in New York.

ALICIA ERIAN's first collection of short stories, *The Brutal Language of Love,* is currently out in paperback from Random House. Her first novel, *Towelhead,* will be published by Simon & Schuster in spring 2005. Her fiction has appeared most recently in *Playboy, Zoetrope, The Sun, Nerve,* and *The Iowa Review.* She teaches creative writing at Wellesley College.

MATTHEW FLUHARTY's work has appeared in journals such as *Metre, Poetry Ireland Review, LIT, Notre Dame Review, Poetry Salzburg Review,* and *The Minus Times.* He is the coeditor of *Breaking the Skin: An Anthology of Emerging Irish Poets* (Black Mountain Press, Northern Ireland) and editor of *Way American* magazine (www.wayamerican.com). He was recently the poet-in-residence at New Light Studios and now lives in Boston.

WAYNE GONZALES is an artist living in New York. He is represented by Paula Cooper Gallery, New York and has on view a one-person exhibition at Galerie Almine Rech in Paris through mid-July. His image of the White House in this issue is easier to see from across the room.

SARAH GORHAM is the author of three books of poetry—*Don't Go Back to Sleep, The Tension Zone,* and, most recently, *The Cure,* which appeared in October, 2003. New work has been published in *The Gettysburg Review, Poetry, Virginia Quarterly Review, Southern Review,* and *American Poetry Review.* Gorham is president and editor in chief of Sarabande Books in Louisville, Kentucky.

ZACH HARRIS was raised in North Hollywood, California. He has attended U.C. Santa Cruz, The New York Studio School, and Bard College. He is currently enrolled in the Hunter College MFA program where he enjoys practicing painting, poetry, and philosophy.

JIM HARRISON's most recent novel, *True North*, came out this spring from Grove Press. His other publications include *Legends of the Fall* (novellas), *Dalva* (a novel), and *Off to the Side* (a memoir). He divides his time between Montana, Northern Michigan, and Arizona.

KATHERINE HOLLANDER graduated from Marlboro College, where she studied poetry and German history. Her poems and critical writing can be found in *Potash Hill*, *The Mind's Eye*, and forthcoming from *The Marlboro Review* and *Poet Lore*. She lives and writes in Ithaca, New York.

LUIS JARAMILLO teaches at The New School Writing Program. This is his first published story. His essay "Big Buck Hunter II" will appear in *Gamers*, an anthology coming out this fall from Soft Skull Press.

DANIEL JOHN, from Saskatchewan, Canada, is a landscape designer. His essays and poems have been published in numerous literary magazines, including *The Comstock Review*, *English Journal*, and *Phi Kappa Phi Forum*. He has ten children.

JANET KAPLAN's two poetry collections are *The Glazier's Country*, winner of the 2003 Poets Out Loud Prize from Fordham University Press, and *The Groundnote*, winner of the 1997 Alice James Books New England and New York competition. New work has appeared or is forthcoming in *American Letters & Commentary, Denver Quarterly, Hotel Amerika, Sentence, Interim,* and *Barrow Street,* among others. She teaches poetry and creative writing at Hofstra University.

JENNIFER L. KNOX was born in Lancaster, California—crystal meth capitol of the nation, and home to Frank Zappa, Captain Beefheart, and the space shuttle. Her first book *A Gringo Like Me* is forthcoming from Soft Skull Press in spring 2005. Her work has appeared in the anthologies *Best American Poetry* (2003 and 1997), and *Great American Prose Poems: From Poe to Present.* She is the cocurator of the Pete's Big Salmon poetry reading series in Brooklyn.

GIUSEPPE O. LONGO is professor of information theory at the electronic engineering department of the University of Trieste. He has done research in network theory and algebraic coding, specializing in coding for finite memoryless and Markov sources. In 1998 he published a book on the cultural effects of the Internet, *Il nuovo Golem*. Longo has published three novels and six collections of short stories as well as numerous texts for radio and stage. In 1996 his novel *L'acrobata* was published in France by Gallimard, receiving the Laure Bataillon award for best novel translated into French. As an actor, he has taken lead roles in plays by Ionesco and Pinter.

CAMERON MARTIN lives and works in Brooklyn. He is represented by Artemis Greenberg Van Doren Gallery, New York. In his first curatorial effort, for this issue he has organized a group of images by artists adapting traditional representational genres to a contemporary perspective.

CHAD McCRACKEN, first out of North Carolina and then Texas, is now a lazy lawyer and occasional philosophy lecturer in Chicago.

DAVID MENDEL is very old indeed. He did so badly in school that he was considered unsuitable for further education. He entered his father's millinery business, and was delighted at the outbreak of World War II as it enabled him to escape into the army. After an undistinguished military career, he took advantage of the British equivalent of the G.I. Bill to take up medicine because he couldn't think of the name of any other profession. He became a cardiologist, and at retirement did a degree course in Italian, which led to a career as a translator.

NADINE NAKANISHI was born in Santa Monica and grew up in both the U.S. and Switzerland, where she currently lives. She has done deck design for Project Skateboards, sculptures for *The Face,* and design and editorial work for *Realrocker, Bail,* and *Monster*.

DAWN RAFFEL is the author of a story collection, *In the Year of Long Division*, and a novel, *Carrying the Body*. She's at work on a new collection.

THOMAS ROBERTSON was born in Minneapolis, Minnesota where he currently lives with his wife and two cats. He has lived in Dover, New Jersey and New Orleans, Louisiana. He's currently working on a comic book about dreams, miscalculated aspirations, and coffee.

RICK ROFIHE is the author of *Father Must*, a collection of short stories published by Farrar, Straus & Giroux. His fiction has appeared in *The New Yorker*, *Grand Street*, and *Epiphany*. A recipient of the Whiting Writer's Award, he teaches writing privately and at the Gotham Writer's Workshop in New York City.

MATTHEW ROHRER is the author of *A Hummock in the Malookas*, which won the 1994 National Poetry Series and was published by W.W. Norton; *Satellite; Nice Hat. Thanks.* (with Joshua Beckman); the audio CD *Adventures While Preaching the Gospel of Beauty* (with Joshua Beckman); and *A Green Light*. His latest collaboration with Joshua Beckman was a ten-hour, nonstop, improvised poem performed overnight at the Bowery Poetry Club, New York City, in May.

SALLY ROSS is an artist who lives in New York City.

GEORGE RUSH is an artist who lives in Brooklyn. He has had recent solo exhibitions with Elizabeth Dee Gallery, New York, and Kevin Bruk Gallery, Miami. His next show, at Galerie Mikael Andersen, Copenhagen, will result from an upcoming two-month residency in Denmark.

HARVEY SHAPIRO is the author of eleven books of poetry, including *How Charlie Shavers Died and Other Poems*, which was published by Wesleyan University Press in 2001. His anthology *Poets of World War II* was published by the Library of America in 2003.

NINA SHOPE received an MFA from Syracuse University in 2003. Her work has appeared in *3rd Bed*. She is a past resident of the Millay Colony for the Arts and has recently completed a collection of three experimental novellas, entitled *Hangings*.

PETER NOLAN SMITH learned how to drink growing up Yankee Irish in Boston and to cook soft-shell crab for twenty from a Virginian mistress. He has ridden a motorbike through Tibet, leapt off a balcony to fight skinheads, been jailed in Paris for graffitiing the British Embassy with a love poem, and ordered Jean-Michel Basquiat to wipe off all the drawings he'd just created on Smith's fridge. He has been a substitute at Southie High during the 1974 bussing riots, run a bar for a Hamburg pimp, traded diamonds on New York's West Forty-Seventh Street, skirted the film business in L.A., and been employed as a "physionomiste" at nightclubs across the world. He currently lives in Pattaya, "the Last Babylon" with his wife and adorable six-month-old daughter.

JAMES C. STROUSE is a writer and cartoonist from Goshen, Indiana. His screenplay, *Lonesome Jim*, was recently made into a feature film, directed by Steve Buscemi, starring Casey Affleck and Liv Tyler. His first published story appeared on *Nerve* and in *The Best American Erotica* 2004. This is his second published story.

WENDY WALKER is the author of the underground classic of science fiction, art history, and espionage, *The Secret Service*, as well as two volumes of tales, *The Sea-Rabbit, or, The Artist of Life* and *Stories Out of Omarie* (all from Sun and Moon Press). *My Man and Other Critical Fictions* is forthcoming from Green Integer. "Sophie in the Catacombs" is from her novel-in-progress, *The City Under the Bed*.

J. PATRICK WALSH III is the third John Patrick Walsh in the John Patrick Walsh family. He is the first to pursue drawings, skateboarding, poetry, stories, videos, and performance in his family. He goes by his middle name Patrick. He is six and one half inch feet tall and is studying at The School of the Art Institute of Chicago. He was born August 7, 1981.

WILLIAM WENTHE has published two books of poems, *Not Till We Are Lost* (Louisiana State University Press) and *Birds of Hoboken* (Orchises). His poems have appeared recently in *Georgia Review*, *Southwest Review*, *Smartish Pace*, and forthcoming in *The Paris Review*. He lives in Lubbock, Texas.

AVA WOYCHUK-MLINAC's poem, "Why?" was composed on February 17, 2000 after a reading at KGB Bar in New York City. The writer was seven years old at the time.

MATVEI YANKELEVICH's translations of Daniil Kharms have appeared in *3rd Bed*, *Open City*, *PAJ*, and *New American Writing*. He has poems in *Carve*, *Weigh Station*, *Fell Swoop*, *Lit*, *Fulcrum*, *New York Nights*, and online at *Can We Have Our Ball Back*, *Shampoo*, *3am*, and *Aught*. Matvei is the editor of the Eastern European Poets Series from Ugly Duckling Presse, and coedits *6x6*, a poetry periodical. He teaches at John Jay College of Criminal Justice.

CHRISTIAN ZWAHLEN is a graduate of Boston College. He lives with his wife in Rochester, New York. This is his first published story.

OPEN

Stories by Mary Gaitskill, Hubert Selby Jr., Vince Passaro. Art by Jeff Koons, Ken Schles, Devon Dikeou. Of the two eggs on the cover, one has cracked. (Vastly overpriced at $200, but fortunately we've had some takers. Only nine copies left.)

ISSUE # 1

Stories by Martha McPhee, Terry Southern, David Shields, Jaime Manrique, Kip Kotzen. Art by Paul Ramirez-Jonas, Kate Milford, Richard Serra. (Ken Schles found the negative of our cover girl on Thirteenth Street and Avenue B. We're still looking for the girl. $25)

ISSUE # 2

Stories by Irvine Welsh (his American debut), Richard Yates (from his last, unfinished novel), Patrick McCabe. Art by Francesca Woodman (with an essay by Betsy Berne), Jacqueline Humphries, Chip Kidd, Allen Ginsberg, Alix Lambert. Plus Alfred Chester's letters to Paul Bowles. (Very few copies left! $25)

ISSUE # 3

Stories by the always cheerful Cyril Connolly ("Happy Deathbeds"), Thomas McGuane, Jim Thompson, Samantha Gillison, Michael Brownstein, Emily Carter. Art by Julianne Swartz and Peter Nadin. Poems by David Berman and Nick Tosches. Plus Denis Johnson in Somalia. (A monster issue, sales undercut by slightly rash choice of cover art by editors. Get it while you can! $15)

ISSUE # 4

Change or Die
Stories by David Foster Wallace, Siobhan Reagan, Irvine Welsh. Jerome Badanes' brilliant novella, "Change or Die" (film rights still available). Poems by David Berman and Vito Acconci. Plus Helen Thorpe on the murder of Ireland's most famous female journalist, and Delmore Schwartz on T. S. Eliot's squint. (Sold-out! Band together and demand a reprint.)

ISSUE # 5

CITY back issues

The Only Woman He's Ever Left
Stories by James Purdy, Jocko Weyland, Strawberry Saroyan. Michael Cunningham goes way uptown. Poems by Rick Moody, Deborah Garrison, Monica Lewinsky, Charlie Smith. Art by Matthew Ritchie, Ellen Harvey, Cindy Stefans. Rem Koolhaas project. With a beautiful cover by Adam Fuss. (Only $10 for this blockbuster.)

ISSUE #6

The Rubbed Away Girl
Stories by Mary Gaitskill, Bliss Broyard, and Sam Lipsyte. Art by Jimmy Raskin, Laura Larson, and Jeff Burton. Poems by David Berman, Elizabeth Macklin, Stephen Malkmus, and Will Oldham. (We found some copies in the back of the closet so were able to lower the price! $25 (it *was* $50))

ISSUE #7

Beautiful to Strangers
Stories by Caitlin O'Connor Creevy, Joyce Johnson, and Amine Wefali. Poems by Harvey Shapiro, Jeffrey Skinner, and Daniil Kharms. Art by David Robbins, Liam Gillick, and Elliott Puckette. Piotr Uklanski's cover is a panoramic view of Queens, shot from the top of the World Trade Center in 1998. ($10)

ISSUE #8

Bewitched
Stories by Jonathan Ames, Said Shirazi, and Sam Lipsyte. Essays by Geoff Dyer and Alexander Chancellor, who hates rabbit. Poems by Chan Marshall, Lucy Anderson, and Edvard Munch on intimate and sensitive subjects. Art by Karen Kilimnick, Giuseppe Penone, Mark Leckey, Maurizio Cattelan, and M.I.M.E. (Oddly enough, our bestselling issue. ($10)

ISSUE #9

Editors' Issue
Previously demure editors publish themselves. Enormous changes at the last minute. Stories by Robert Bingham, Thomas Beller, Daniel Pinchbeck, Joanna Yas, Adrian Dannatt, Kip Kotzen, Geoffrey O' Brien, Lee Smith, Amanda Gersh, and Jocko Weyland. Poems by Tony Torn. Art by Nick Stone, Meghan Gerety, and Alix Lambert. (Years later, our cover photo appears on a Richard Price novel.) ($10)

ISSUE #10

OPEN

CITY back issues

I wait, I wait.
A brilliant outtake from Robert Bingham's *Lightning on the Sun*. Ryan Kenealy on the girl who ran off with the circus; Nick Tosches on Proust. Art by Allen Ruppersberg, David Bunn, Nina Katchadourian, Matthew Higgs, and Matthew Brannon. Stories by Evan Harris, Lewis Robinson, Michael Sledge, and Bruce Jay Friedman (tall, Jewish, with good table manners). Rick Rofihe feels Marlene. Poetry by Dana Goodyear, Nathaniel Bellows, and Kevin Young. ($10)

They're at it again.
Lara Vapnyar's "There Are Jews in My House," Chuck Kinder on Dagmar. Special poetry section guest edited by Honor Moore, including C. K. Williams, Victoria Redel, Eamon Grennan, and Carolyn Forché. Art by Stu Mead, Christoph Heemann, Jason Fox, Herzog film star Bruno S., and Sophie Toulouse, whose "Sexy Clowns" project has become a "character note for [our] intentions" (says the *Literary Magazine Review*). See what all the fuss is about. ($10)

I Want to Be Your Shoebox
Susan Chamandy on Hannibal's elephants and hockey, Mike Newirth's noirish "Semiprecious," an excerpt from Eileen Myles' memoir, *Inferno*. Rachel Blake's "Elephants" (an unintentional elephant theme emerges). Art by Viggo Mortensen, Alix Lambert, Marcellus Hall, Mark Solotroff, and Alaskan Pipeline polar bear cover by Jason Middlebrook (we're still trying to figure out what the bear had for lunch). ($10)

SUBSCRIBE
One year (3 issues) for $30; two years (6 issues) for $55 (includes a free totebag). Add $10/year for Canada & Mexico; $20/year for all other countries.

TOTEBAGS
Natural-colored cotton totebags with a nice long strap and a navy blue Open City logo. Only $5 for this fashion essential!

T-SHIRTS
Nice, black, 100% cotton T-shirts with white type, with **OPEN CITY** on the front and ALWAYS OPEN on the back.* Available in men's medium, large, x-large, or women's medium (tight, girlie-style). Only $15.

*T-shirt concept by Jason Middlebrook.

Please send a check or money order payable to:

OPEN CITY, Inc.
270 Lafayette Street, Suite 1412, New York, NY 10012
For credit-card orders, see www.opencity.org.

OPEN CITY
READING SERIES

PAST, PRESENT, AND FUTURE
READERS INCLUDE:

Jonathan Ames • Betsy Andrews • Nico Baumbach • Daphne Beal • Joshua Beckman • Thomas Beller • David Berman • Jill Bialosky • Rachel Blake • Paula Bomer • Michael Brownstein • Annie Bruno • Sam Brumbaugh • Heather Byer • Angela Cardinale • Bryan Charles • Craig Chester • Emily Clark • Marcelle Clements • Susan Connell-Mettauer • Susan Chamandy • Tom Cushman • Adrian Dannatt • Eric Darton • Gabriel Marc Delahaye • Mary Donnelly • Lesley Dormen • Dahlia Elsayed • Alicia Erian • John Epperson • Jack Fitzgerald • Bruce Jay Friedman • Josh Gilbert • Jesse Goldstein • Daniel Greene • Dana Goodyear • Elizabeth Grove • Christopher Hacker • Evan Harris • Noy Holland • Mira Jacob • Luis Jaramillo • Ryan Kenealy • Hunter Kennedy • Alix Lambert • Jessica Lamb-Shapiro • Heather Larimer • James Lasdun • Sam Lipsyte • Nick Mamatas • Matt Marinovich • Ann Marlowe • Donna Masini • Vestal McIntyre • Martha McPhee • Jim Merlis • Honor Moore • Carolyn Murnick • Eileen Myles • Maggie Nelson • Arthur Nersessian • Mike Newirth • Daniel Oppenheimer • Michael Panes • Vince Passaro • Daniel Pinchbeck • Mark Jude Poirier • Sarah Porter • Greg Purcell • Andrea Reising • Rebecca Reynolds • Matthew Roberts • Rick Rofihe • Matthew Rohrer • Saïd Sayrafiezadeh • John Seabrook • Eric Schlosser • Ryan Schneider • Harriet Shapiro • Harvey Shapiro • Jeff Sharlet • Nina Shope • Peter Nolan Smith • Sabin Streeter • Jean Strong • Toby Talbot • Bill Talen • Nick Tosches • Lara Vapnyar • Jack Walls • Charles Waters • Paolina Weber • Amine Wefali • Rachel Wetzsteon • Jocko Weyland • Tim Wilson • Carlin Wragg

AT KGB BAR AND BOWLING GREEN PARK, NYC

**SEE WWW.OPENCITY.ORG FOR INFORMATION
ABOUT UPCOMING READINGS.**

ELK

"You may ask yourself after
checking it out,
'but what does it all mean?'
And, well, if you have to ask
you will never know"-*Thrasher*

www.elkzine.com

Marine Pvt. Arthur A. Leyrer w/Blowfish, South Pacific, U.S. Marine Photo, 1943

ART INTERNATIONAL 2004

6th ART FAIR

15 - 17 OCTOBER 2004

CONGRESSIONAL CENTER ZURICH

Daily 10 - 20 h

International Fair for Contemporary Art

INFORMATION

BB International Fine Arts GmbH
Infoline   0041 55 420 33 05
E-Mail   info@art-zurich.com

WWW. ART- ZURICH.COM

Rice Manhattan
227 Mott Street
212.226.5775

Rice Brooklyn
81 Washington Street
718.222.9880

Low (bar below Rice)
81 Washington Street
718.222.1LOW

www.riceny.com

His goal was obscurity

but he kept blundering into sense.
(Shapiro, page 209)

North

Jason Brown

REBECCA SAWYER WAS THE FIRST PERSON FROM VAUGHN TO score a perfect 1600 on the Scholastic Aptitude Test. When the news hit the *Valley Journal*, Mr. Sumner, her advisor, who had always said she was honors material and who had recommended on more than one occasion that she aim for state college, maybe for elementary education because she seemed to have the patience to work with children, marched her by the arm into his office. She had never been one of the best students in the class, not even in the top ten, but Mr. Sumner was also the boy's basketball coach, and Rebecca knew that in his world, where people were either starters or substitutes, she had just been called off the bench. He spoke to her with half-time urgency. He flattened his hands on his desk and shook his head. He called her young lady. He was incredibly excited, he said, about her future.

Rebecca couldn't see how a score a few hundred points one way or the other could have much of an effect on anyone's future when five years before a girl from Fort Kent, near the border of Quebec, had scored 1550, only to become a veterinarian's assistant.

"That's Fort Kent," Mr. Sumner said, pointing to his right at a bookcase lined with trophies. "*This*," he said, tapping his desk, "is Vaughn."

In the hall outside his office, a group of junior girls stopped talking as Rebecca walked by on her way to the bathroom where she stood alone in front of the mirror looking at herself. Next to the morning's article about her scores, the paper had printed a photo of her at the kitchen table. She had large dark eyes, dark hair, and a round face. Some people said she looked Italian or Portuguese; everyone agreed she looked nothing like her parents, grandparents, cousins, or aunts. The bell rang for the beginning of the next period but she kept staring. Some part of her was speaking to some other part of her, deciding something without her permission.

On her way into Mr. Cunningham's U.S. history, she accidentally slammed the door and felt everyone look up as she crossed the room to her assigned seat by the window. Mr. Cunningham continued talking, referring to the reading from the night before while pointing to the board with yesterday's quizzes held curled in his fist. He asked what had happened in 1865, and looked from her to the left side of the room and back to her. Mention of the year brought the text before her mind as if onto a screen, the words scrolling down through her thoughts. She rarely spoke in class, but now, she felt, Mr. Cunningham and the other students waited for her to confess that she had always known the answers.

Rebecca's grandmother, Grandmame, was dying very slowly of old age, and every afternoon before dinner Rebecca spent a few minutes in her small room off the kitchen, which smelled of the hall closet and of burnt dust from the electric heater Grandmame turned all the way up. According to Rebecca's mother, it would have been cheaper for them to build their own power plant.

Rebecca sat in the green chair and looked with her Grandmame through the window across Central Street to the Methodist Church and told her, as she did every day, how school went and what boys she liked. She made up the names of the boys.

"I thought of something to tell you," Grandmame said, "and now I can't remember. Well."

Grandmame removed her hand from Rebecca's and gripped the arm of her chair as if she were about to pull herself up.

"Have you heard anything from your brother?" Grandmame asked, and Rebecca shook her head. Grandmame asked this all the time, and the answer was always no. She dozed off again, her hands folded in her lap.

No one was allowed to speak of her brother in the house, except

Grandmame, who did whatever she wanted. Even so, Grandmame always spoke about Jeremy in a whisper. Usually in the same breath she added that Rebecca's mother was cold. Everyone needed someone to blame, Rebecca supposed.

Jeremy's last visit, three months ago, had ended with a scene in the kitchen Rebecca would never forget. She didn't know how it started, or what the argument was about, but suddenly their mother's face turned red and she started screaming obscenities at the top of her voice. Jeremy's face drained for a moment, with his eyes closed, as if he had left his body, and then he flew through the air to punch their mother so hard in the face that her nose exploded with blood. Before Rebecca could even be sure what had happened, Jeremy ran out the door.

When he arrived home from work, her father cursed and threw his bag onto the kitchen table. "He can't keep running," he yelled from the living room where he stood looking out the window toward the river. He said he thought Jeremy had probably hopped the train and gone north, as he had the last time he ran away, to a tiny place called Dennis where he knew people. Her father said he didn't think there was much up there now, since the end of the seventies when they stopped driving logs down the river. Maybe abandoned loggers' camps and old farms. Probably squatters.

"I remember what I wanted to tell you," Grandmame said as Rebecca sat up. Rebecca thought it might be something new this time, even though Grandmame often got worked up over things she had just talked about the previous day. Rebecca was the only one who listened, and the only one Grandmame usually wanted to talk to.

"Not long after I was married to your grandfather, we bought this farm from a family who had seen trouble. I forget what kind now, money trouble. We gave them a good price I think, but they needed to sell in a hurry, so I believe we paid less than we might have."

Rebecca had heard this before and felt annoyed for a moment. The story went along as usual: the family they bought the house from had a daughter who died, and they came to Rebecca's grandparents asking to bury the girl in the graveyard. Their family had lived on the land for a hundred years. But Rebecca's grandfather said no.

Grandmame leaned over as if she believed this was the first time she

3

was telling Rebecca the story. Each time her Grandmame told it she reminded Rebecca not to tell anyone, not even her parents.

"One afternoon I was working in the abandoned garden when I found a patch of loose ground. I dug deeper with the trowel until I hit something hard. I thought it was a stone. That ground was full of stones when we bought the place. But when I cleared the dirt away, it was a girl's face. There was dirt in her mouth over her teeth, and over her eyelashes. Her skin was half rotted away. The smell was just the most horrible thing I had ever known. I went into the house for a sip of your grandfather's whiskey."

Grandmame paused, shaking her head. It seemed as if she was catching her breath to continue. Rebecca tried to think of something to say to stop her from going on.

"I covered her up. I put my garden on top of her. What else could I do? If I told your grandfather, he would have dug her up. I'm the only one who knows she is there." Grandmame's face trembled slightly, and her eyes watered.

Rebecca rested her hand on Grandmame's arm. There was no girl buried in the ground. According to Rebecca's mother, the story had been circulating around the town for a hundred years, made up by the man who had owned the *Valley Journal* at the turn of the century as a Halloween tale for his daughter and her friends. It had been reprinted several years before to mark the anniversary of the paper.

In the field behind the house the morning light pinched Rebecca's eyes and seemed to sap her strength. She dressed and walked outside carrying her shoes. Wet grass slid between her toes; the sky at dawn had been orange, she could tell, from the white haze still on the horizon. The air held still for a moment over the farm, waiting for the late morning breeze to sweep up the valley from the ocean. Maybe it would be warm, or the clouds might roll back from the coast. She stood there until the breeze came up, sending the maple and oak leaves into a boil. She was waiting, but she didn't know what for.

The school sat on top of the hill, its windows dark, as if no one was there, though she knew everyone was already in first period, lined up in rooms watching the teachers. Rebecca's friend Kathleen waited for her outside the front doors, in the usual place. Kathleen didn't care about being the smartest girl in school, she didn't even take the

S.A.T., but Rebecca couldn't be sure how much would change between them now.

"I was about to give up on you," Kathleen said. "Smartest girl in school and she doesn't know what time it is." Kathleen shook her head disapprovingly. Rebecca started to apologize, but Kathleen raised her hand. "I always knew you were smart. Nothing you can do about it."

Rebecca was relieved that Kathleen thought being smart was a simple characteristic, like having hideous toes, that shouldn't change anything. And maybe in the past this had been true. Rebecca's father had told her that Grandmame was extremely smart, though you couldn't tell now. He described a time when he was young and his father was lecturing Grandmame on what was true and not true in state politics. She had embarrassed him after church by disagreeing with him in front of his friends. They were walking through the church parking lot, Grandmame yanking Rebecca's father along by the hand as her husband told her what was what. When they reached the end of the parking lot, Grandmame began reciting numbers at the top of her voice. At some point, Rebecca's father realized that Grandmame was listing the license plate numbers of all fifty cars in the church parking lot.

Rebecca's English teacher, Mrs. Lucas, called her up front after class and congratulated her, smiling thinly. Several other teachers did the same thing, but none of the students said anything at all. On the surface nothing changed, but people in the lunchroom seemed quieter when she passed, and when she sat down in the corner next to Kathleen, no one looked over at them. It wasn't what people would say, Rebecca realized, it was what they wouldn't say—even the teachers—as they tried to act naturally. Even Kathleen measured her words as she told a story about her boyfriend David's car breaking down. They were afraid now—of what, she couldn't be sure. Maybe of what she was thinking.

After school, while her mother was out shopping and her father at work, Rebecca wandered through her parents' bedroom looking at the old pictures of her relatives, most of whom she had never met. She found a portrait of her grandfather standing outside the old barn in his overalls, frozen in that single moment. She sat down on the edge of her parents' bed and looked at a picture on the wall of her brother Jeremy when he was five, leaning over the porch with his face covered in jam. In another picture, at their uncle's wedding, he stood at six years old in a blue blazer and yellow tie, already wearing their father's face. Five years older than her, he had always done things with her rather than make friends with boys his age. It was more of a problem when she started to make friends of her own, and didn't always want him around. She felt guilty about that now, and wanted to take each of those moments back. She remembered one time when she was six or a little older. They were down at Boynton's Market, and Jeremy asked what she thought would happen if their parents both died. She was eating ice cream; it was summer. She didn't answer, had never thought of this before. Jeremy must have seen she looked worried because he told her not to worry. He had it figured out. They would be fine. He knew exactly what they would need and how they would get it.

"You promise?" she said.

He said of course, and then she made him promise again because he had always said that one promise meant nothing but two meant you couldn't get out of it.

The first time her brother ran away after a shouting match with their mother he was sixteen. He came into her bedroom the night he left and sat on the floor running his hand down the length of his face. She was afraid to move as he rose on his knees as if he was going to pray.

"I don't know where I'll be." He whispered so lightly she wasn't even sure he wanted her to hear.

Even though he hadn't asked her to, she promised she would come find him, and then she promised him again.

A few hours before dawn, it started pouring outside Rebecca's window. She had gone to bed early with an upset stomach, without eating dinner. She stood and pressed her forehead against the cold glass, looking into the backyard, and was not surprised that Jeremy wasn't leaning against the well house as the drops thudded against the hollow gutters. For a long time she had not wanted to admit that she knew things others could not know. It wasn't just about facts anyone could look up in a book. Now that the article had come out in the paper, everyone would suspect that she knew too much. For instance, the photo of her grandfather in her parents' bedroom had been taken in 1955—she knew he was thinking of China Lake where he had grown up swimming with his two brothers. He was thinking of the lake because it was the tenth anniversary of his younger brother's death in the war. She knew this from looking into the photograph, into his dark eyes half hidden behind his sagging lids. And she knew what her father would never admit, even to himself: that he no longer loved her mother; and she knew that her brother was going to die.

She didn't have the strength to move or say anything when her mother called up the stairs an hour later and then came to sit on the edge of the bed resting the back of her hand against Rebecca's cheek.

"You're burning up," her mother said. "I'll call."

Rebecca knew she wasn't sick—she just couldn't stop thinking, which was a sickness no one could fix—but she went along to the doctor's office where, in the waiting room, her mother flipped through a *Good Housekeeping*, snapping the pages so fast she could not even have been looking at the pictures. Every time the door to the nurse's area opened, her mother looked up, startled, until finally she slammed the magazine shut and swore. "Jesus." She looked at her watch and folded her hands in her lap. Her mother often spoke to herself. She called it her therapy.

Rebecca stared wearily at her mother until her mother looked up and shuddered.

"What?" her mother asked. "What are you looking at?" She stood up officiously and came over to sit next to Rebecca and feel for her temperature again. "You're still burning."

"I'm not sick," Rebecca said.

Rebecca followed the nurse to the examining room. When he arrived, the doctor's greeting was hollow, echoing across the distance between his lips and his attention. Rebecca had heard him saying goodbye to the previous patient. She closed her eyes and opened her mouth so he could examine her throat, and every muscle in her body seemed to relax.

"You had a fever last night and this morning?" he asked. She nodded. His breath brushed her neck as he leaned over to look inside her head. He asked her to tilt her neck slightly and she did. He rested a hand next to her leg on the table and pressed his fingers against her neck below her jaw.

He told her she might have a small infection but didn't think she needed antibiotics, at least not yet. In the car her skin seemed to vibrate where the doctor had touched her, like a trivial memory that would not go away, and when her mother asked, Rebecca told her what the doctor had said.

"For that," her mother replied, "we pay him."

Once, when no one else was around, Rebecca's father had said of her mother that she would never let them forget she was from Portland.

Rebecca told herself there was no point in going—she could not change what would happen—yet she had to. She waited until early morning. Her father had said Jeremy jumped the train and rode it all the way up to Dennis, so that's what she would do.

In the hours before dawn, the train moved slowly in the heavy air, the lights from Water Street flashing between boxcars. As she had seen boys from school do, she ran along a granite wall that paralleled the tracks and jumped up on the floor of one of the cars, landing in the cool inside where the clicking of the metal wheels amplified in the empty drum. The train followed the river for ten or twelve miles before crossing over in Gardner and heading north out of the valley into the rich smell of the tidal banks. She leaned against the frame and looked at the black trees in the blue glow of the woods. Only now did she find the tear in the knee of her pants and in the skin underneath, which seemed the only evidence that she had made it this far.

The half moon passed in and out of the clouds, giving brief glimpses of her white sneakers. The train slowed before each town and sped up as it snaked back into the woods where for several minutes she couldn't see the tops of her hands. The air in her chest seemed to vibrate with the floor of the boxcar, turning each breath into a gasp. She would not be able to scream if she had to, and even if she could, no one would hear her above the scraping of the wheels over the tracks. Jeremy must have felt, as she did now, that he was in the grip of an iron fist that would not let go.

She fell asleep curled up and woke to see the train stretching through a bend in the mist. The sun, just struggling through, lit up the rust-red boxcar with BOSTON-MAINE painted on the side. At one crossing a man standing with a paper bag took off his hat and laughed when he saw her. She hung out of the door by her arm and looked up the track where tree branches arched over the train. Finally, she saw a green sign for Dennis. She wasn't moving very fast, but it was frightening to jump and roll in the grass not knowing what lay underneath. She rose to her feet and ran for a dirt road, where she turned just in time to see the caboose rocking on its narrow perch.

A half-mile down she thought she saw a gas station and a store on the other side of the street, but there were no people or cars, nothing to suggest a town. Maybe this was the edge of town and she had jumped too soon. She walked in the direction of the gas station, scuffing her sneakers through the dirt. Part of her hoped she did have the wrong place because if she found him she would have to say something. She never wanted to be the one to speak and hated the feeling of people looking at her waiting for what she would say, for her thoughts, for what she knew. People were greedy. They pretended not to want things, they pretended not to care, except for Jeremy, who never pretended he didn't need anything from anyone. He needed her to look for him.

A truck approached from behind, sending up a plume of dust as the driver steered with his right hand on top of the wheel, his chin pulled in. Messy clumps of hair stuck out beneath his cap. She expected the truck to drive stop at the store, but instead it took a left and crawled over a driveway toward a low farmhouse once painted white and since worn to a rotting gray. She knew Jeremy was inside. It had been this simple for him: jumping off the train, finding an abandoned house. This was the way he did everything, choosing what was in front of him as if there was no other choice.

She stopped walking several times in order to think more clearly, and once almost turned around, though she sensed with resignation that turning around would lead to the same place, in the end, as going through the open front door of the house. A box of rusty tools sat in the front hall and the air felt breathed and rebreathed by the cracked and buckling plaster. A gas can leaned against the wall. In the living room one of two windows opened to the field behind the house where the tall grass bent under a breeze and pushed up again. It seemed impossible that the world outside, where the air moved through the light, was at all connected to the world inside this house, and it wasn't right that she had been able to pass so easily between the two. Jeremy lay on a battered couch with his arms at his sides, his eyes closed. She thought he must be sleeping, but then his eyes snapped open and stared at her as if he didn't know her and she had come to take everything away from him. Small bottles, a plate, and a leather belt sat on an upturned box at his feet. She said his name, but he did not say her name back or change his expression in any way. When he swallowed, a cleft appeared in his chin and the veins of his neck pushed against his translucent skin. His Adam's apple fluttered as his eyes closed, and his chest rose and fell to the timing of heels clomping down the stairs behind her. When no one appeared, she thought the pounding had come from her own head, but the man she had just seen in the truck stepped from around the corner with his hands in his jeans pockets, the leather cap on his head. He quickly removed his glasses to clean them on his T-shirt. He said he was hoping she would come by.

"How do you know who I am?"

"How did you know which house to walk into?" He put the glasses back on and looked at her. He was probably her brother's age or a bit older. He sat in the chair next to the couch, crossed his legs, and rested his chin on his hand. His sharp lips chopped off the consonants when he spoke, sounding to her like one of the migrant worker's kids.

"I'm not from around here like my friend," he said, as if this should explain any questions she might have. He leaned back and clasped his hands behind his head with his elbows in the air.

"You're not his friend!" Rebecca shouted in what could not have been her voice.

"Whatever you say." He shrugged one shoulder and glanced over at Jeremy who seemed to see through them. "We've got everything you need here to be happy. We've got food if that's what you need, we've got money, we've got a roof that don't leak—and we've got *business* coming right down from Canada. This here's a stop on the trans-Canada highway." He looked at her brother for a moment before turning to her and reaching in his jacket pocket to pull out a photo in which she thought she could see her brother and herself when they were younger, but she quickly looked away and shook her head. She couldn't breathe.

"That's my favorite picture," he said, saying it *pi-sure*, while looking away, as if embarrassed. He sighed and dropped his shoulders into the silence that followed and lasted until he seemed smaller than her. "That's at Niagara Falls. I've never been there, but I want to go, I plan to go. In fact, I could go right now if I wanted to. There's nothing stopping me."

"I have to go," she said and then watched him, waiting to see if he would try to stop her.

"Suit yourself." He closed his eyes and slid further down in the chair.

Jeremy turned to face the wall, and she opened her mouth to call out to him—if she just said his name, maybe he would come back with her, though of course he wouldn't. If she said his name, he might explode, as he had that morning at her mother. He didn't want to attack her—the idea would never occur to him—but whatever pushed from the inside against his rising and falling back hated everything, even her.

Outside, she ran across the overgrown field for the road and the tracks, stopping only to catch her breath and look over her shoulder. No one followed. Everywhere she looked, down either direction of the tracks or across the field into the woods, she saw the starved image of Jeremy's face. She ran for a few more minutes, stopping when she could no longer breathe to bend over her knees and make a sound in her throat like the wheels of her father's car crunching over their gravel driveway.

A train would come eventually, if she kept walking in the direction of home, and if she kept her thoughts straight and parallel to the glinting edge of the rail, which drew her under a canopy of turning leaves. The tips of her sneakers slid forward over the chattering gravel until she was convinced the noise came from Jeremy or the other one following her, and she started to run again until she reached a bridge over a river.

She thought she saw something moving through the trees to the right but instead of going back or freezing (as she told herself to do), she ran toward it, jumping over fallen trees and yelling Jeremy's name. She stopped in a clearing above a stream and looked around, but there was nothing there. The blue sky paled around the edges. Pockets of warmth drifted in the cool air. She looked down the slope, feeling as though she could see inside the wind brushing through the grass. The distant pines leaned together in a sudden gust and were still again. When the breeze returned, it seemed to whistle through her limbs, and she realized that Jeremy had been here, in this clearing, in the grass. He had measured the wind by the movement of the branches.

The train whistle bleated as it passed through Dennis, and she bolted toward the sound. The wheels ground against the rails, ticking off what little time she had left to get home before they knew where she had gone and what she had seen. The boxcars moved through the trees, speeding up as if the forest was rushing south. Some of the Boston-Maine cars were empty, doors sliding back on both sides, the sunlight blinking through the openings as she ran to the bridge and there jumped from a railing half onto the edge of a car. Inside, with her face pressed to the cold metal, she sensed him: Jeremy's face with the stranger's hat and long arms, both of them in the same body standing in one of the dark corners. She looked for their smile, and their eyes, glowing in the shadow, but there was nothing.

The train slowed into each town, the tracks occasionally winding within fifteen feet of kitchen windows and the backyards of houses she passed. It was not hard for her to determine the characters and even the thoughts of the people living inside. People wanted you to think things were complicated when they weren't. Through a window a woman looked up from doing the dishes. She's thinking about her twelve-year-old son, Rebecca thought, who was caught stealing from a corner store. All the information was in the air around her, waiting for her to absorb it. Her mother was frightened and vain; she always had been and she always would be. Her father was patient and simple near the surface and unhappy underneath. It couldn't be any different than the facts she learned for tests: Pablo Picasso, born October 25, 1881. His first painting, *La fillette aux pieds nus*, 1895. A poem she glanced at two weeks before, the "Song of Apollo," with the second stanza, *Then I arise; and climbing Heaven's blue dome, I walk over the mountains and the wave . . . I am the eye with which the Universe Beholds itself, and knows it is divine.* The Earth was formed 4.6 billion years before. The words cesium, curium, erbium, rhodium, argon, osmium, streamed through her head faster than the trees whipping by outside.

She remembered a story her mother told of being a girl in the 1950s and traveling on a freighter across the Atlantic to Europe with her father, who was a merchant marine. There was a storm—a hurricane, her mother had said, and described the ship rising up the mountainous waves, the wind faster than if you put your hand out of the window on the highway. Her mother had been much younger than Rebecca was now, and as her mother's father helped on the deck of the freighter, she sat alone in the dark cabin. Rebecca had heard her mother tell this story dozens of times over the years, and each time her mother stuck out her chin and wore a blank, put-upon face. Each time, Rebecca mistook her mother's expression for boredom, as if she was being forced to tell the story again even though no one had asked her to. Now Rebecca could see the expression was thinly disguised pride. Rebecca's father realized this, too, which was why he complained every time that it wasn't actually a hurricane. "All right, it *wasn't*," her mother shouted at him one night in front of people from his work who were having dinner at their house. She stood up from the table with tears in her eyes. "It wasn't, okay, it wasn't *officially* a hurricane if that makes you happy. I was ten years old down in a square metal room with no lights or windows and with the boat practically upside down back and forth for eighteen hours!" Her mother turned and left the table but came back in a moment to apologize and laugh lightly. "My, my," she said when she sat, refolding her napkin. "You'll have to excuse me."

Her mother had been terrified in that room, holding onto the edge of a metal bunk as everything lurched back and forth and the inner workings of the boat groaned. When Rebecca closed her eyes, she could see her mother clinging in the dark compartment with no idea if they would survive or if she would see her father again. The noises of the ship would not have been much different than the noises of the boxcars knocking together as she sped through the woods.

The crossing bells chimed one after another as she drew closer to Vaughn, and she expected someone she knew, a friend of her mother or her guidance counselor, to look up from their gardening or their steering wheel to see her face in the open door of the boxcar. When she leapt from the train onto the grass near the town library, she expected the bell at the Catholic church up the street to ring for the six P.M. service or the Baptist church for their seven P.M. service or at least the more distant sound of the town hall clock bell sounding on the hour. But it wasn't Sunday night, there were no services, and it wasn't on the hour. She sat on the grass watching the train pick up speed as it left town, the lights of the caboose fading into the darkening pines, and the crossing bells growing silent one after another in the distance.

In the kitchen, the heat from her mother's cooking clung to her cheeks and palms.

"I put all the dish towels in the laundry. Would you grab me one from upstairs?" her mother asked. Rebecca nodded.

"You're home late."

"I was at Kathleen's."

"Hurry up and wash your hands and you can help me set the table."

Her mother took the forks and spoons, moving back and forth deftly between the stove and the table with the same urgency she brought to every night's dinner.

"Okay," her mother said after everyone sat, reaching out to take Rebecca's and Grandmame's hands. "Someone say grace, please."

As Rebecca's father started, her mother squeezed her hand so hard the bones of her fingers pinched together. Her mother pulled her jaw in and cinched her eyes shut, tears welling up over her bottom lids and washing down her face. She always feels so much, it's as if she feels for all of us, Rebecca thought.

"I think I'm coming down with the flu," her mother said. "I'll go lie down for a while." She plucked her hands away from them and stood up from the table as if from an insult.

"Do you want one of us to come with you, with some food?" her father asked. "There is something going around at work. Maybe you have it."

Rebecca knew from the tone of his voice that he didn't think she had the flu, and that he had no intention of comforting her.

"Go ahead and eat," her mother said.

Grandmame stared across the room for a few minutes while Rebecca's father unfolded his napkin and arranged his silverware in a perfect row.

"Don't let your mother's hard work go to waste," he said as he started cutting into the pork chop. After a few more minutes, after Grandmame had started eating, humming faintly to herself, as she sometimes did, a tune no one recognized and which probably wasn't a real song at all, her father leaned back and asked Rebecca what she had done at school that day.

"Nothing," she said.

"Nothing?" he said, raising his eyebrows. "Well, that's good. They're getting you used to the working world. You've got three and a half hours—less a coffee break or two—of nothing before lunch, but you don't want to use it all up before lunch because you've got a good four of nothing after lunch. And then you want to be careful to have people see you shove nothing in your briefcase at the end of the day so they think you're doing nothing at home, too." He smiled through this, amused with himself.

Grandmame went back to her room while Rebecca helped her father carry the dishes to the sink. He scraped the plates that she handed to him and stacked them neatly in one side of the double sink with the silverware piled in a basket. She was just turning back to the table for the salad bowl when he started humming a song she didn't recognize. He caught her arm and pulled her toward him, swaying from left to right in a dance he must have learned before she was born—she had never seen him dance. A smile spread up from his chin until his whole face lifted, and he opened his eyes and chuckled before letting go, turning off the water, and picking up the *Valley Journal* from the counter on his way to the living room.

"What about the rest of the dishes?" she asked.

"Leave them, I'll do them later," he said, raising the back of his hand, though she knew he wouldn't. "Go check on your mother."

Her mother lay on top of the covers in the dark bedroom, her arms spread wide, and her eyes closed. Rebecca thought she was asleep.

"Come here," her mother said, holding her hands out like a child wanting to be picked up. Rebecca pulled back at first but then held her hands out. Her mother's crying passed up into her own arms and across the back of her neck.

"He's not coming back, is he?" her mother said. "It's going to be winter soon—it will be so cold up there."

"Of course he's coming back," Rebecca lied, tumbling forward from the weight. Her mother wrapped an arm around her shoulder and squeezed as she buried her face in Rebecca's neck. The smell of her mother's hair was both familiar and distant, like the sight of her brother's face, and the harder her mother squeezed the more Rebecca felt as if she were far away from this moment, floating over their house and town.

"Please, promise me you won't ever become mixed up with the people your brother did."

"I won't," she said.

"Of course you won't," her mother said. "You're too smart for that."

Her mother rolled onto her back, lifted her hand to her forehead, and sighed. Rebecca waited for what she would say—when her mother lost control, she talked frantically afterward to cover it up.

"I don't know why I was thinking about your brother tonight," her mother said. "Before dinner I was remembering a trip your father and I took right before we were married, when I was already pregnant with your brother. Your father's mother didn't even want us to get married, I don't suppose there's any harm in telling you now—because I wasn't Catholic—and she did not approve of taking a trip like this before the wedding, but the wedding was in the fall—it had to be, I forget why, I guess because I was already pregnant. I don't know how we thought we were going to fool that woman. The trip was on an old tall ship, up the coast. We sailed for ten days, with three other couples. Every evening before dusk the captain and the crew anchored in a small harbor, and while they put everything away and made us supper, we sat on the deck and looked out at the ocean. We had absolutely nothing we had to do. I knew it would be rare in the life we were starting, but your father, who had worked on the farm from the day he started walking until he started college, couldn't understand why anyone would want to sit still for so long staring at the sky and the water. I think the whole thing was torture for him. One evening before dinner, he stood up beside me, stripped down to his boxers, and dove off the bow. It was as if he just couldn't sit still any longer and he had to make some work for himself. Watching the bottoms of his feet disappear, I just lost it for a moment. It was stupid, but I thought he wouldn't come back up—that he was running away from me. This time on the boat was the longest we had ever spent together, and I felt this desperation of not wanting to lose him. When I saw him crash up a little ways out, shivering and waving with a big smile on his face, I was so happy, I almost jumped in after him, and I probably would have if that water wasn't cold enough to stop your breath forever."

Her mother fell silent with her arms at her side. Her toes and fingers twitched after a few minutes as her breath settled into the rhythm of sleep. Rebecca listened for her father's footsteps, but she could tell from the distant flutter of a turning page that he was still down in the living room reading the paper.

She stared at the bedroom ceiling and imagined standing with her mother as her father swam back to the boat and climbed up the ladder. Her father dressed, hopping on one leg, and whispered something in her mother's ear as she bent over, laughing. Rebecca had never seen her mother laugh this way before. Her parents put their arms around each other and walked toward the stern as if Rebecca wasn't there because, of course, she wasn't. Then her father ran back toward her, but only for his jacket, which lay at her feet, and when he glanced up, there was no look of recognition on his face. Rebecca knew this feeling, had known it all along, of not being seen, but she would also remember the look on her father's face that told of how even this brief moment away from his new wife was too much to bear.

Rebecca went to bed, falling immediately asleep without undressing, and didn't know what time it was when she sat straight up and looked out the dark window. Her clock radio was unplugged, probably from when her mother vacuumed, and her limbs felt heavy as she wandered down into the kitchen. The moon hung low in the sky, everything silent except the dormant sounds of the house, the refrigerator, the furnace in the basement.

"Rebecca, is that you?" her Grandmame called from her room. Even though her Grandmame rose before dawn, she kept the blinds tightly drawn at night and the room pitch black, so that Rebecca had trouble finding her way to the ratty green chair.

"Is that you?" Grandmame said again. She was only a foot away in her narrow bed, but Rebecca couldn't see her face.

"It's me," she said.

"There was something I wanted to tell you after dinner, but I didn't get the chance."

Instead of going on, though, her Grandmame's breathing calmed, and the airless room filled with the musk of her skin and clothes.

Rebecca leaned her head back and pictured herself on the train headed north toward Jeremy. She tried to remember his face in that house but could only see the strain of his neck and the cleft where there had not been one before. The harder she tried to remember his face, the more he looked like someone she didn't know. She thought of what her mother had said about winter coming. In one afternoon, everything she had seen up there—the pines, the field, and the low house—would be sheeted white against a white sky. If he was still in Dennis, he wouldn't stay there for long, she guessed, and he wouldn't come back to Vaughn. He would continue north on the train hundreds of miles through the thick forest until there was nothing but rock covered with ice. She pictured him there, as far up as anyone could go, walking across a blank white plain extending out to the horizon. Her brother, she realized, had gone north not to run away from life, as her father had said, but to know everything. Because he had wanted her to follow, she would have to keep looking for him, even if she would never find him, and even if he was no longer there but somehow everywhere, all around them.

Grandmame shook Rebecca's leg, and Rebecca opened her eyes to the morning light framing the shade.

"An awful, awful thing has happened," Grandmame said in such an urgent voice that Rebecca leaned forward to hear. But then Rebecca realized her Grandmame was about to tell the tale, once again, that she had read in the newspaper of the girl who had been buried in a backyard. There was nothing Rebecca could say to stop her Grandmame, so she just listened and waited for the story to end.

"*I* was only six years old when they buried me," Grandmame said as tears soaked the moth wings of her cheeks. "My father wanted to put me next to his mother, but the people who bought the farm from us wouldn't let him, so he dug my grave in their vegetable garden while they were sleeping, and no one knows. No one knows where I am."

The train whistle blew in the distance, the first warning of its approach from the north. Rebecca felt the air shiver from the force of the locomotive against the tracks as the second whistle blew and echoed down the valley, carried south by the tide. The third whistle blew the final warning, though to Rebecca it was less a warning than a cry.

"I don't want to be buried in this place," Grandmame said and squeezed hard on Rebecca's arm. "Promise me you won't let them."

A promise was easy to give, and as Rebecca whispered it, Grandmame sighed as if she had finally been relieved of an unbearable secret.

I'd never been a Mexican before and now I was. (Jaramillo, page 85)

Saving the Daylight

Jim Harrison

I finally got back the hour
they stole from me last spring.
What did they do with it
but put it in some nasty cold storage?
Up north a farm neighbor wouldn't change
his clocks, saying, "I'm sticking with God's time."
All of these people of late seem to know
God rather personally. God even tells
girls to limit themselves to heavy petting
and avoid the act they call "full penetration."
I don't seem to receive these instructions
that tell me to go to war, and not to look
at a married woman's butt when she leans
over to fetch a package from her car's
backseat. I'm enrolled in a school without
visible teachers, the divine mumbling
just out of earshot, the whispering from the four million
mile an hour winds on the sun. The dead rabbit
in the road spoke to me yesterday, also the owl's wing
in the garage likely torn off by a goshawk.
In this bin of ice you must carefully
try to pick the right cube.

Adding It Up

Jim Harrison

I forgot arithmetic but does one
go into sixty-six more than sixty-six times?
There's the mother, two daughters, eight dogs,
I can't name all the cats and horses, a farm
for thirty-five years, then Montana, a cabin,
a border casita, two grandsons, two sons-in-law,
and graced by the sun and the moon, red wine
and garlic, lakes and rivers, the millions of trees.
I can't help but count out of habit, the secret
door underneath the vast stump where I founded
the usual Cro-Magnon religion, a door
enveloped by immense roots through which one day
I watched the passing legs of sandhill cranes,
napping where countless bears have napped,
an aperture above where the sky and the gods
may enter yet I'm without the courage to watch
the full moon through this space. I can't figure
out a life. We're groundlings who wish to fly.
I live strongly in the memories of my dead dogs.
It's just a feeling that memories float around
waiting to be caught. I miss the cat that perched
on my head during zazen. Since my brother died
I've claimed the privilege of speaking to local rocks
trees, birds, the creek. Last night a broad moonbeam
fell across my not-so-sunken chest. The smallest
gods ask me what there is beyond consciousness,
the moment by moment enclosure the mind

builds to capture the rudiments of time?
Two nights ago I heard a woman's voice from across
the creek, a voice I hadn't heard since childhood.
I didn't answer. Red was red this dawn
after a night of the swirling milk of stars
which came too close. I felt lucky not to die.
My brother died at high noon one day in Arkansas.
Divide your death by your life and you get
a circle though I'm not so good at math.
This morning I sat in the dirt playing
with five cow dogs, giving out a full pail of biscuits.

Easter Morning

Jim Harrison

On Easter morning all over America
the peasants are frying potatoes
in bacon grease.

We're not supposed to have "peasants"
but there are tens of millions of them
frying potatoes on Easter morning,
cheap and delicious with catsup.

If Jesus were here this morning he might
be eating fried potatoes with my friend
who has a '51 Dodge and a '72 Pontiac.

When his kids ask why they don't have
a new car he says, "these cars were new once
and now they are experienced."

He can fix anything and when rich folks
call to get a toilet repaired he pauses
extra hours so that they can further
learn what we're made of.

I told him that in Mexico the poor say
that when there's lightning the rich
think that God is taking their picture.
He laughed.

Like peasants everywhere in the history
of the world ours can't figure out why
they're getting poorer. Their sons join
the army to get work being shot at.

Your ideals are invisible clouds
so try not to suffocate the poor,
the peasants, with your sympathies.
They know that you're staring at them.

Endgames

Jim Harrison

Within the habit of prayer it's hard
to drop the names of those already dead,
the same with the address book
where you don't want to cross out names
just in case they might decide to return.
Bettors call this the world's longest shot,
but then we can't abandon our dreamscapes.
Yes, I was at a mountain lodge in Chiapas
with Penelope Cruz where the creeks ran uphill
carrying lazy waterbirds to their mountain home.
"Jim," she said, "I can only give you one more day.
I don't like the way you float out
the window as if your blood was helium
and the kinky demand that I sit
naked on the cusp of the new moon.
Just settle down and be like an ordinary
street-car conductor in Seville." But as a fish
I'm always thirsty forgetting that I live in water.
Penelope leaves before dawn fatigued
with all of the old flowers in my mouth.
She'll see me if I go to Granada, dig up
the bones of her countryman Lorca, and bring
him back to life. This morning, I can't quite
do this for myself. I am dreamt.

I Want You to Follow Me Home

Christian Zwahlen

ONE NIGHT AT AROUND EIGHT O'CLOCK THE PHONE RINGS AND a boy asks if Party Girl is there and you hang up on him because you don't like the way he says it.

You're eleven years old, and your sister, Mary, is fifteen. And U2 has just come out with the song "Party Girl," and it's sort of popular with people your sister's age. And some of them have started calling her that. As a nickname.

"Who was that, Mark?" your father asks.

"Prank call," you say. But you're lying and your father knows it. He works as a lawyer for a big insurance company. He knows when people are lying.

Your father is always flying to Detroit and Connecticut and Florida on business, and when he gets home at night he just likes to relax. He just likes to take off his suit coat and sit there in his suit pants and tie and a pair of slippers, and smoke cigarettes while watching a hockey game on TV. He has olive skin. Your family is Lebanese. Lebanese-American.

When the phone rings again that night your father yanks the receiver from the wall.

"Hello," he says, hollering over the noise of the hockey game.

"Who?" he says. His face is wrinkled. He pinches his cigarette between the thumb and ring finger of his left hand. He slips one of his feet in and out of his slipper as he listens. He's wearing brown socks.

Very slowly he says, "Who. The fuck. Is this?"

And then he listens for another moment and slams the phone back in place. And you jump.

"Who the hell is Party Girl?" he says. And he stares down at you.

That summer your family goes to Cape Cod for three weeks. Every morning you get up early and head to a hot, white beach, where you spend most of the day. On Sundays you go to Mass first and then the beach. Some time just before low tide each day, a sandbar emerges about a hundred yards out in the water. And your father and Mary and you swim out to it. It's always cooler out there. There is wind and it is wet. There are sand pipers herding themselves through the wide, warming puddles of seawater.

One day you are out there on the sandbar and Mary says, "Dad?"

And your dad says, "Yeah, sweetie." He is trying to relax, but you don't think he is having a good time of it. He is chewing his mustache and his knees are sunburned.

"Can I go on a date tonight?" Mary says.

Your father takes off his sunglasses and looks at Mary. He looks spaced out. The skin under where the sunglasses have been is pale and sweaty.

"A what?" he says.

"A date."

"I heard you," your father says, and puts his sunglasses back on. "With whom?" he says.

"A boy."

"No."

"Dominic his name is," Mary says.

"Dominic what?"

"Dominic Crowe.

"Dominic Crowe," your father says. "From where?"

"I don't know. Leominster."

"Dominic Crowe from Leominster," your father says. "I never heard of him."

"They own a house here," Mary says.

"Does he have a car?"

"Yes."

"Then no," your father says.

"Daddy," Mary says. You have buried your feet in the wet sand and are trying to stare directly into the sun. A seagull screams overhead.

"No."

"Please?"

"No."

At 7:30 that night your sister Mary walks into the saltbox Cape house your family is renting and introduces you all to a tall, skinny, tow-headed boy who looks way too old for her.

Your mother has been shucking corn. Your father is fixing himself a drink.

"Well, hello," your mother says.

"Daddy," Mary says, "this is Dominic Crowe from Leominster."

Your father is wearing khaki trousers and a V-neck T-shirt. He looks at Dominic Crowe. Then he wipes his right hand on his trousers, and holds it out to this boy. It hovers between them for a moment, like some kind of threat. And then, finally, Dominic Crowe takes your father's hand. He tugs at it once and lets go. Your father leaves his hand there and looks sort of hurt. He grabs his drink and takes a long, slow sip and stares down at Mary.

Mary is wearing short khaki shorts and a bikini top. She has flip-flops on. But it looks as though she hasn't been wearing anything on her feet all day because the bottoms of them are dirty.

"Well, hello," your mother says again, breaking the silence.

Dominic Crowe then speaks up. "I'd like to," he says, "I'd like to take Mary out."

Your mother smiles and you zero in on her teeth. They are very straight, and small, and white. Except for her canine teeth, which are pale yellow. She sometimes looks at them in the mirror and calls them her coffee teeth. You stare at your mother's teeth because you don't want to make eye contact with your father, who looks angry. Or with Mary, who looks desperate. Or Dominic Crowe, who looks dumb. And old.

The ice in your father's glass rattles.

"I already told you no," he says, and walks into the living room.

Your mother frowns, and so you can't see her teeth anymore.

You hear your father sit down on the plastic-covered sofa and click on the TV with the remote just before he bellows, "Noooo."

Dominic turns and walks fast to the screen door. He lets it slam instead of holding it for Mary, who is right behind him. He lets it slam in her face. Her hair puffs away from her head when the wind from the door hits it.

After dinner that night Mary says she is going for a walk and you follow her down the road. You stay about fifty yards behind her.

"Stop following me, Mark," she says.

There is no sidewalk so you walk on the shoulder. After a while Mary starts to run. And then you run. There are cars out on the main road and it feels dangerous. There's sand in the road.

"Stop," Mary screams at you in front of the sandwich shop.

But you keep following her. You don't want to let her get away. You try to hold something in your head. A fragile sort of emotion. But it keeps pulling away, like the seawater on the beach.

Mary runs far ahead to the Cold Harbor Beach parking lot and then she runs into the dunes. And you can't keep up with her. And you can't find her in the dunes.

You walk out of the dunes on the beach side and walk along the water. And then it starts to get dark. The light all around you is soft and blue and gray, slowly deepening into twilight. And then it becomes a deep, blue gray. You walk up and down the beach, looking for Mary. You're not sure if the tide is going out or coming in, but you know it is doing something. It is moving. Changing. The air smells of the life and death of wet, muddy, salty things. Snails mating, maybe. Or seaweed rotting.

You know Dominic Crowe is in one of the houses perched above the beach. And that maybe Mary is in there, too. You hear voices. Groups of people at a party. You see lights and moths. There have been coyote sightings on the beach. And it's dark. And you want to go back to your mother and your father.

The lights shine in the houses above the beach. They have wood shingling and are very large. They look nice. There are moths crashing into the brightly lit windows.

You head for the dunes, deciding to make your way back to the parking lot and the road. It's cool in the dunes in the dark. The sand emanates a coolness up onto your feet and around your ankles and calves. You think that the sand kind of shines coolness. A kind of cool, black glow. It makes you think of snow for some reason. And water. All that cold water.

Coming through the dunes there are shadows. You smell dog shit for a moment and then that passes and you are relieved. Relieved that you haven't stepped in anything.

There is a pale, blue streetlight humming in the beach parking lot. It brings light and shadow into the dunes. You are at the very edge of the dunes, coming into the parking lot, and there you find Mary sitting on one of the parking logs.

She is smoking a cigarette, which you have never seen her do before. She has a beer between her legs.

She is all alone. You think maybe she'll start crying, but she doesn't. She just stares off. She doesn't have her flip-flops on anymore and when she stretches her legs out you notice that the bottoms of her feet are still very dirty. She pinches the cigarette between the thumb and ring finger of her left hand.

She looks just like your father.

You walk up next to her and stop.

She smiles.

The streetlight makes you both look pale blue. Except for your hair and eyes and the bottoms of Mary's feet, all of which are dark blue like the night.

"I told you to stop following, Mark," Mary says.

She closes her legs tight around the beer can.

"Yeah, but I wanted to," you say, and she just looks at you.

"I was out on the beach," you say.

She sees you see her beer.

"Were you up at one of those houses just now?" you ask.

"Yes," she says.

"At a party or something?"

"Yep," she says.

"With that boy?"

"Yep."

"Is that why they call you Party Girl?" you say.

"No," she says. "It's just a song, Mark. It's a song by U2."

"I know," you say. "But it's not just a song. It means something else, too."

Mary smiles again. Dark blue lips and pale blue teeth. Then she frowns. Just like your mother.

"What does it mean?" you say. "That you go to parties with people like that boy?"

Mary doesn't say anything.

"And you drink and stuff?" you ask.

"Yep," Mary says. "And other stuff."

"Why do you want to be called Party Girl?" you say. And Mary is quiet. "Do you? Do you want to be called Party Girl?"

Mary considers this for a moment. The ocean sounds very loud on the other side of the dunes. You think maybe the tide is starting to come in.

"I don't know," Mary says. "I just am."

You want to comfort her somehow, but instead you decide to reach between her legs and take hold of the beer can. She lets you take it and you lift it and drink from it and then toss it into the dunes. It's the first time you've ever littered at the beach. That and the beer make you feel powerful and old. But Mary just laughs at you.

"Don't laugh," you say, and the two of you stay there like that for a moment. Just looking.

"I want you to follow me home," you finally say.

And you start walking across the parking lot toward the road. And Mary does too. She follows you. She follows you across the pale blue sand of the parking lot, and onto the dark blue gravel of the road. And the walking. The walking ahead with Mary walking behind. The sound and the weight of your bodies as you walk. The cadence of it. The sound of your feet on the sand and stone. It's like an embrace for you. A warm, blue embrace.

Recurrence of Childhood Paralysis

Priscilla Becker

The dog lay dead in the backyard for days
and I sacrificed a doll to keep
him company in the earth.

The mulberry trees, which I have mentioned,
dropped hot fruit.

That nostalgia followed me,
a negligent strain—imprecise and unhappy.

The ground is sere
as though a jar had covered it.

A little like a lazy eye, I'd been
not precisely where I seemed.

I hope you are imagining my childhood.

Like sleeping, it was once described to me,
but knowing that you sleep. Once I wanted
very much to say I love you—that,
but bodily.

Blue Statuary

Priscilla Becker

The songs wore out; they rusted
the radio. The singers began to die.
I left my toenails at the beach, hoping
they would grow another body.
I would return with a better,
more expressive face.

I loved it when you said my name.
When you didn't, I listened
to the sounds the world made.
The trees especially injured me,
though they wouldn't have known.
When the wind arrives, it upsets them.

I would return with sand in my hair.
The silence, I expected.

It's time to go out on your own.

J. Patrick Walsh III

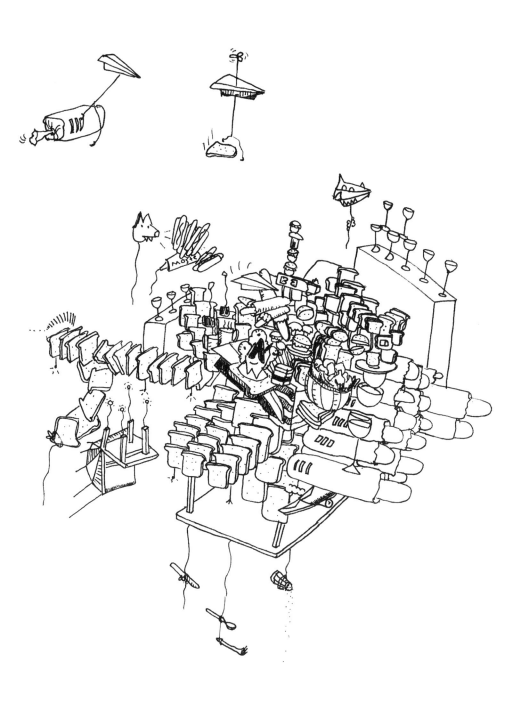

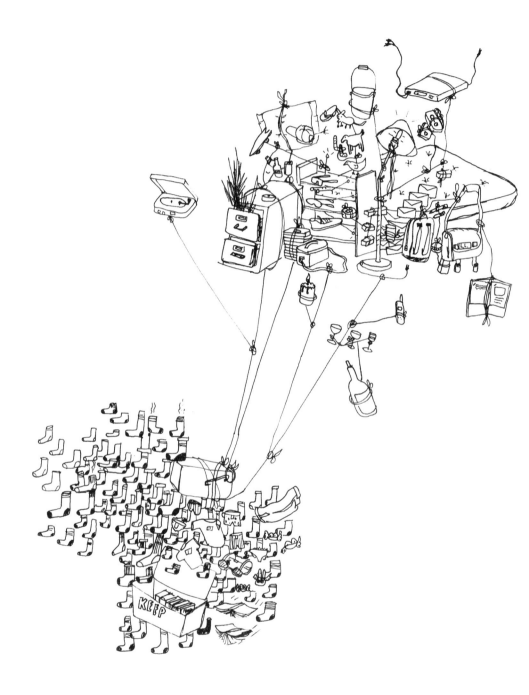

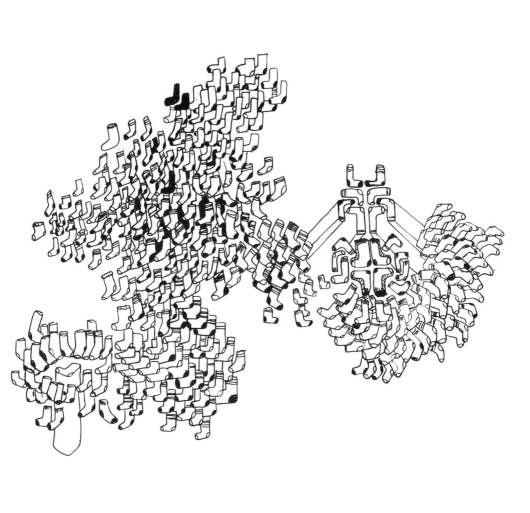

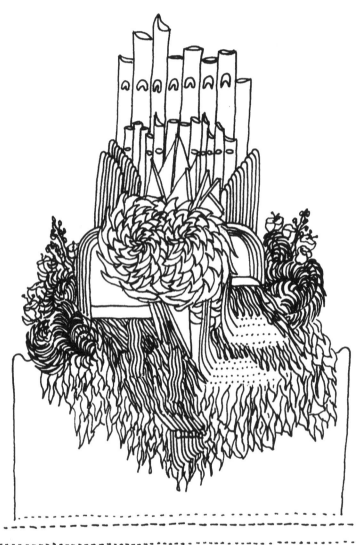
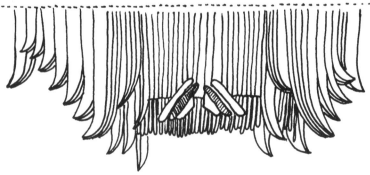

Dollar Movies

Bryan Charles

IT'S EARLY SENIOR YEAR, STILL PRETTY MUCH SUMMER, A SATURDAY night. The Judy Lumpers have just finished a set at Dick's Basement, the little club in Quincy, and I'm sulking in the shadows, agonizing over the usual botched chords and some of my more embarrassing unreached vocal high notes, when a girl, a stranger appearing from nowhere, tells me how much she likes my band. Here's a first, I'm thinking. If you believe mythology, or have read the biographies, every guy who picks up a guitar is only trying for the snapper. But really, groupie-fucking is the province of the more decadent hard rock and hair bands, from Guns N' Roses, say, all the way down to every aspiring burn-out who plays Peppers, the venue for shitty metal in Kalamazoo. Anyway, the girl introduces herself as Molly and says, "What's that one song, the one about, like, the tattered tongue of an otter?"

"That's called 'Tongue.' But the line you're thinking is really 'the tender tongue of autumn heat.'"

"Oh," she says. "I like that one."

"Thanks," I say.

"Tongue" is okay, not one of our finest hours, the riff lifted almost whole cloth from the Sonic Youth song, "Sister." Plus, I never believe anyone except Jake and Wheeler—the Judy Lumpers' bass player and drummer—who says they like our songs.

The only beverage Dick's sells is Faygo Red Pop, so Molly and I tip a few and shoot the shit while the next band sets up. She goes to

Quincy High, the Gull Lake rival in matters of sport, and she loves the Doors. She shows me a small tattoo on her ankle, the initials JDM, meaning James Douglas Morrison.

"I got it last year. My parents don't know yet. This summer I covered it up with Clearasil and my Doc Martens."

"Then what's the point?"

"Well, just to know that Jim's here, that he's a part of me. Do you think that's corny?"

"No, not at all," I say. This is the heart-shaped erection at the center of my brain talking.

The band starts playing and it gets too loud to talk, so we go for a walk on the train tracks that run through Quincy, follow them past the edge of town, out into nothing, out where it's as though Molly and I are the only two people alive, wandering the earth just because. A breeze rolls in off the cornfields all around us and the air goes from mild and a little muggy to cold and crisp. The temperature drops ten degrees in one second. I've never felt anything like it. Molly stops and crosses her arms. "Where'd that come from?"

"I don't know, but it feels good."

"Do you want to hug for a second, just to warm up?"

"Okay. But I was sweating at the show. A little warning," I tell her.

"That's all right."

I take a deep breath, put my arms around her. The silence that follows makes me self-conscious, so I say, "Like this?"

"Yeah," she says. Then, "Wow, you really do stink."

"I tried to tell you," I say, pulling away. Molly pulls me back.

"But it's not terrible. It smells like, what, like fried onions." She moves her head so she's looking up at me, the eyes saying, Do it, fool, but I can only stare dumbly at her mouth. I need clearance, a guarantee. To go in for a kiss and have the girl pull away is one of my most crippling fears.

"Can I kiss you?" I say.

She smiles and nods, the green light, and I'm grinning back, still as a fucking statue. Molly says, "Were you going to do it tonight or . . . ?"

"Yes, tonight." I lean in and we do it, we kiss. The styles are nice and soft, no forceful probing tongue. Her fingertips brush against my cheeks, my heart stutters, charges faster, like being shocked back to life on the operating table.

Five minutes later we're dry humping in the grass by the train tracks, and I'm picturing gruesome war photos, like piles of bodies in the Nazi death camps, like the Vietnam guy taking a bullet in the brain, to help contain the explosion forming below. When it gets really close, I stop humping and say, "Let's take a little break."

This works okay until we roll over and she's on top. Now I'm helpless, almost a spectator, watching her move against a backdrop of ice-chip stars, the big black sky, the universe expanding around us, her long brown hair falling across my lips, eyes, nose. And then it happens, what feels like every second of human existence charges out of me and into my underwear.

I stop moving again, too embarrassed to say why.

"Are we taking another little break?" she says.

Luckily, a train comes along, a speeding Amtrak, its horn blasting away the question, and I don't have to answer. I get so scared when it roars by that I jump up and sprint into the woods, tripping over a dead branch and falling on my face in the process. It's kind of nice down here among the dirt and the ancient leaves and I contemplate not answering when I hear Molly call my name. But she finds me, she looks down at me and says, "How could you be so afraid of something you knew was coming for miles?"

When I stand up she takes my hand.

For our first real date we rent *The Doors*, which Molly says she's seen at least ten times, four on video, six in the theater. She tells me it's the sexiest movie ever made.

"There's something about Oliver Stone movies. They radiate sexiness. With Jim Morrison it's easy, because he's so fucking sexy, but even something like *Platoon* has erotic qualities."

"*Platoon?*" I say. "What are you talking about?"

"I'm talking about the part where Willem Dafoe dies. It's so tragic that it actually ends up being sexy, the way his body shudders when he gets shot. Very orgasmic. Plus there's a little glimpse of Johnny Depp during the village massacre scene."

I think of my anti-coming death fantasies and say, "What about *Born on the Fourth of July?*"

"I know it's not cool to like Tom Cruise, but I think he's really sexy, even in that. He's in a wheelchair, he's got a mustache, he's an alcoholic.

But that part where he's screaming the word 'penis' at his mom. Look out."

"*Wall Street*?" I say.

"*Wall Street* is the least sexy Oliver Stone movie, if only because it stars Michael Douglas, who I've found repulsive since *Fatal Attraction*. God, his flat, flabby butt when they're in the kitchen."

Her house is small and her bedroom is between her parents' and little sister's rooms. The make-out options aren't great. There's the basement, but the walls and floors are paper thin and I haven't felt secure there since the time we heard her parents whispering through the vents about what do you think they're doing down there, why are they being so quiet?

So we go to the East-Towne 5, the dollar theatre in Kalamazoo, and we buy tickets to random movies, kissing and groping in the back row like desperate middle-schoolers, hardly glancing at whatever's on the screen. And it hits me at some point that this is where I want to be when the world ends, here with Molly in the dark, dust rising through the projector's beam, listening to some lame comedy or second-run blockbuster while our hands get sweaty from constant holding and I taste her lips, her Junior-Minted lips.

Times are so fine at the East-Towne, our secret haven, that I leave the movies insanely depressed. I cling, sit through every word of the credits to the copyright date, then stumble back into the world like a coma patient who wakes up wishing he'd stayed asleep, or better yet, slipped away forever. Then it's off to the Denny's on Sprinkle Road, for black coffee and french fries with guacamole, and no matter how long we sit there, Molly and I, free associating on caffeine highs, the end is always the same, a little kiss in the driveway, nothing heavy, and she's out the door of the car.

In my secret thoughts, I feel relief. I don't want the pressure of trying to be a top sexual performer, someone like my Uncle Bro, who when I was younger and he lived in our basement, said to me, "Vim, if you ever want a girl to fall in love with you, you better learn to eat a pussy so good it sings back 'The Star-Spangled Banner.'"

We're parked in Molly's driveway after seeing *What About Bob?* for the second time in three days and the goodnight kiss gets longer and longer until the windows fog and our seats are back. I put my hand on her belt buckle, thinking, hoping, she'll stop me, but she doesn't. I undo the buckle and the top button of her jeans.

Down goes the zipper.

"What if your parents are watching?" I whisper.

"They're not," she says.

I stop and clear a little porthole in the fog, look through it to the darkened windows of her house. "How do you know?"

"Because it's midnight, because they're sleeping."

"What about your sister?"

"She's eleven, she's asleep, now come here."

"I can't. I can't get on top of you, there's the gearshift there, I don't think my legs will fit."

"Just stop talking and everything will be fine."

I look at the house again, then back at Molly. I put my hand on her stomach, move it to the edge of her underwear, thinking, What now, will someone please fucking tell me what now?

Her eyes are closed. When I slip my hand under the elastic, she smiles. It's barely there, a Mona Lisa smile.

This is my left hand, my fretting hand. It can form seventh and ninth chords, the jazz chords, can make beautiful noise without me looking or thinking. But it's like there's a mannequin hand on the end of my arm now, some bloodless thing, as I feel, for the very first time, a girl's pubic hair and the dream underneath.

I press into the wetness and rub gently around and for a long minute, forever, nothing happens. Then Molly starts breathing faster. She squeezes the armrest on the passenger door. I watch her hand squeezing the armrest. I move my finger up a fraction of an inch and she gasps.

"Shit, sorry," I say. "Shit. Are you okay?"

She laughs and the sound of her laughter makes me want to pop a suicide capsule. "What? What's so funny?"

"Nothing," she says. "Shhh."

Her hand over mine, guiding me back into the wilderness. I'm concentrating so hard sweat drips into my eyebrows and a mild headache blooms and wild lightning flashes of the past and future ricochet around the inside of my skull. I imagine Molly's parents peering out at the car, feeling helpless and disappointed, imagine being asleep later in my bed and how I'll think of this moment ten, twenty, thirty years from now, imagine my father performing similar acts on my mother in the days before they realized they didn't love each other anymore, imagine almost everything except what's happening now.

Molly releases her grip on the armrest and I panic, try frantically to find whatever I'd found before. Nothing. Her breathing becomes more and more relaxed until it's like she's watching a filmstrip in science class. I pull my hand away, she zips and buttons her jeans. We both move our seats up. "Anyway," she says.

I start the car and turn on the defroster. "I'm sorry," I tell her.

She shifts toward me. "What for?"

"I don't know," I say after a few seconds.

"Sorry is something you shouldn't say unless you know why."

"What if you don't know why but you mean it anyway?"

"Then you've got some kind of a problem."

"Sorry," I say again.

In a single motion she kisses me on the side of the mouth and opens the door. "Call me tomorrow."

On the way home I sniff repeatedly at my finger. I roll down the window, stick my face out, and scream into the early October darkness. I put in an Afghan Whigs tape and sing along with their songs of sexual conquest, trying with all my heart to feel triumphant.

The next day, Saturday, Jake and I go to his brother's apartment in Kalamazoo and spend the afternoon sucking down a case of Old Milwaukee. I was already feeling blue about my lackluster sex abilities, and it only gets worse with a buzz. The more beers I have, the more every thought becomes a picture of Molly's disappointed face, or what I think her face would look like disappointed.

"What the fuck's your problem?" says Gary, Jake's brother, when he sees me sprawled on the living-room floor.

"It's chicks, man, the ladies."

"I know what you need, little soldier." He goes away and comes back holding two shot glasses of brown liquor. "Down the hatch."

After that I take a long walk and end up by Waldo Stadium, where the WMU Broncos play. It's a home-game day and I wander among the big crowds of tailgating students, feeling like something they vomited out of their happy faces.

There should be a pill for when you're with a girl and the lights go out. And I don't mean a contraceptive. I mean something that gives you knowledge of the tender places and dulls the fear.

Just as I'm thinking this, some guy yelling "Go Broncos!" shoves a cold Bud Light into my fist. I drink it down and the world looks stupider.

Back at the house I take the cordless phone into the bathroom and dial Molly's number. "Please," I say when I hear her beautiful voice, "give me one more shit. I mean, chance."

"Who is this?" she says.

I burp into the phone. "It's me, Vim Sweeney."

"Vim? Are you drunk or something?"

"That's right. Just like Jim Morrison, your favorite poet of the darkness." Silence. "I am a dark poet," I say.

"What does that mean?"

"It means I'm not afraid of death or dying," I tell her. "Do you hear me?"

"No. Not really. I'd kind of like to know what the hell you're talking about."

"I'm talking about can I come over?"

"I don't know. I guess so. I mean, my parents are here."

"So let them hear our passion through the vents. I'll just stop off first, at the place, and I'll get that box of rubbers."

She laughs uncertainly. "Vim, this is . . . you're being really weird."

"Ribbed, for her—I mean, your—pleasure," I say.

There's a long pause. I can hear the party noise below, can feel the music going into my feet. I step into the shower. "You should try and get some sleep or something," Molly says. Her voice sounds very far away. "Try and sober up. You're not driving are you?"

"Not yet, but I will be as soon as I get off the phone."

"Don't do that. Stay wherever you are and we can talk some other time."

"Do you love me?" I say. No answer. I slap the tile and ask again.

"Vim, I think I'm gonna go."

I sit all the way down in the tub to stop the spinning. "Great," I say.

"So I'll talk to you later."

"Great."

The line goes dead, the dial tone comes on. It's the loneliest sound I've ever heard in my life and I can't fucking stand it, so I press redial.

"Great," I say when she answers.

"Now you're annoying me," Molly says. "Seriously."

"I lied before," I say.

"About what?"

"I don't really like your tattoo."

"Bye, Vim." She hangs up again.

I pass out for a while, until Gary kicks in the door. "There you are, little soldier," he says over the sound of his piss splashing.

"Where have you been?" Jake says downstairs. "What are you doing?"

"I'm making mistakes. I think Molly and I just broke up."

"Molly? Wow. I didn't even know you were going out," he says.

"We are. We were." I feel like I've been sleeping in that bathtub all night, but when I look at the clock I see it's barely ten.

An hour or so later, somewhat sober after a few cans of Jolt, I get in my car and drive to Meijer's Thrifty Acres, where I pick out a single red rose, the best one I can find, from a cooler in the House and Garden department. Then I take the long way home, Kings Highway, stop off first in Quincy. I circle Molly's block a few times and finally park down the street. There's a long row of pines leading up to her house and I sneak through its shadow, feeling like Ted Bundy, until I'm almost in the yard. All the lights are off except the blue TV glow in the living room. I stand there a long time, staring at the spot where Molly and I parked last night, thinking of the way she breathed during that special little minute when I'd touched her right.

My plan was to knock on her window and give her the rose, an old-school romantic gesture, something I've never tried before, something real, but it's crumbling inside me. All my fake bravery seeps out into the night. The mailbox is just right there, at the edge of the grass. I sprint over and open it, gently lay down the rose, and run back to my car.

Sunday comes and goes. Molly doesn't call and I don't call her. I'm in the middle of failing a geometry test on Monday when I decide to stop by her house after school. I drive around the block again, like last time, going crazy, just like last time. I stand alone on the porch for what seems like an hour. It's cool outside, and very bright, my favorite time of year. I ring the doorbell. Molly answers, but she steps out rather than invite me in.

"There you are," I say. Where else would she be? Her tight, green and white striped sweater gives me a little charge, makes me long for the old times of the East-Towne 5, which were just three days ago. I tell her I'm sorry and she rolls her eyes.

"Vim, you say that about everything."

"I do, you're right, but at least now I know why I'm saying it."

"Well, that's just great," she says. "Great, great, great."

"See, I can accept that. I'm trying to be mature." The wind picks up, just like it did in the beginning. "Are we broken up?" I say.

"I believe we are." It hurts me, ruins me, to hear this, but I can't show it. I can't show anything. None of this would have happened if we'd never left the movies, if we'd died there, like I'd wanted to.

"Did you at least get my rose?" I ask her.

"What rose? What are you talking about?"

"I put a rose in your mailbox."

"When?"

"The other night. Saturday. After I called you."

She glances behind me, looking confused. "The mail doesn't come on Sundays."

"That's true."

"And I don't think anyone got it today."

"Maybe you should get it now."

Together we walk to the mailbox. Molly pulls out a thick stack of mail. As she does this, my crushed, dead rose falls to the pavement at her feet. I pick it up and hold it in the air and say, with the sun blinding me and my hand and that stupid rose both shaking, I say, "For you."

On one of the rural roads, Bibbs noticed a large turtle trying to cross, and hit his brakes. He didn't even pull over—just stopped right there in the road. He hopped out of the car and Rosalie followed him.

"I wish I had my camera," she said.

"You direct traffic," Bibbs told her, even though there was no one coming in either direction. He leaned down then and gripped the turtle's shell on either side, near the back feet. Rosalie thought this might make the turtle tuck its head in, but instead, it extended its neck fully and snapped its toothless jaw in the direction of Bibbs's left hand. All four of its feet were paddling the air, claws extended. (Erian, page 109)

Elsewhere

Jack Anderson

On a day like this,
open and empty,
I feel made of air,
so outside myself
I could be elsewhere,
all becomes elsewhere,
the air is Tulsa,
a city with streets
named after other
cities far away:
Boston, Peoria,
Detroit, and Cheyenne,
streets stretching outward,
open and empty
at this time of day,
no people, no cars,
the buildings rising
like ghosts of buildings,
and the only sounds
are bird calls, church bells,
freight trains, train whistles
whistling out into
this onward outward
of wide empty streets
and their endless miles
of church bells, bird calls,
and freight trains whistling,

OPEN CITY

whistling far away,
and today stays still
other and elsewhere,
open and empty.

Believing in Ghosts

Jack Anderson

1

Two strangers who met while sipping coffee at a sidewalk café started talking about ghosts. "I don't believe in ghosts," said the first.

"Oh really?" said the second, and vanished away.

2

Two strangers at a café were talking about ghosts. "I don't believe in ghosts," said the first.

"Oh really?" said the second, as the first vanished away.

3

Two strangers at a café were sipping coffee and talking about ghosts. "I don't believe in ghosts," said the first.

"I don't either," said the second, and they ordered some more coffee.

4

Two strangers sipping coffee at a sidewalk café were talking about ghosts. "I don't believe in ghosts," said the first.

"I don't either," laughed the second as they both vanished away.

5

Two strangers met over coffee at a sidewalk café. After sipping and chatting they finally agreed, "We don't believe in ghosts," whereupon their cups, the coffee in them, their tables and chairs, and the whole café plus the street around it vanished away, leaving them nowhere but there.

She finished making a boat for no one

and gave it to the water

and walked alone

past houses being built

and houses being torn down

and then she walked where there were no houses

(Robertson & Rofihe, page 213)

Platform

Nina Shope

WHEN THE SUBWAY HITS HIM, HE IS STARING STRAIGHT AT IT AND thinks for a moment that he will be able to embrace it, that the train will simply stop, resting against the bones of his shoulders, the wheels pressing against his knees like a body kneeling, like his body kneeling on the tracks.

The first things to break are his shoulders as it hits his opened arms, body thrown back and under, the rush of noise like the seashore when one is struck by its simultaneous silence and sound. And he is tossed side to side as if under rough surf. The strength of it turning his body, rolling it, like a riptide pulling out to sea. Metal waves. Thick current. Metal tracks. Wheels. He kicks strongly against it. Strikes forward with his hands, thinks that he will be able to pull himself free from the force of it. Surfacing. Holding his breath.

The first things lost are his legs. Sawed through at the thighs, they break the surface, kicking outward from underneath the train's belly. And now he can drag forward with his arms. He takes a breath, turns his head against the noise. The screeching. Gulls perhaps. Metal beaks. Claws. Dull metal eyes. Dumb birds, he thinks. Scavengers. Waving them away. And suddenly the pull stops without any apparent slowdown. One moment it is there and then it has gone. No birds anymore. Just dirty overcast sky. Metal clouds. Darkness. And his face turned against the tracks like the slatted windows he used to peer through as a boy, his mother in the yard, the curve of her back, bending.

His wife stares at the strange space at the bottom of the bed where his body ought to be. Such a sudden foreshortening. And she bends down to look under the bed, thinking that the rest of his body must be there, like a magician's assistant in a box who has supposedly been cut in half.

Under the bed there are tubings. Yellow. Red. Urine. Blood. With a dark tube running between them. He must have hidden his legs somewhere else, she thinks. Eyeing the cabinet in the corner of the room, the bunched shape of the curtains. Clever, she thinks. You can't even see the trick.

In the shows, it is always women in their frilled costumes who are placed inside—the box only large enough for skinny bodies and slender knees. He should have known this—that it is the woman who is sawed through the center and made whole again. Who is tied to the tracks. Rescued. That it was not the place for him—a magician climbing into the box, waiting for top hat and wand. For the feet to wiggle even once the legs were removed. The wand waved over the box—the body come back together again. And she wonders what phrase was supposed to be spoken. What magic password uttered before scalpel and suture began.

Climbing into the bed beside him, her body curls into the space where his is not. And furtively she tries to bend her legs so that her knees join his bandaged thighs, becoming a continuation of his own. But she cannot look at him this way. Hermaphrodite. Red high heels. Slim calves turned sideways, skewed off from the rest of his body. She feels as if she is at a peep show—looking at something through closing windows, closing her eyes against it. She moves quickly away from him and bends to remove her shoes, feeling ridiculously overdressed. Garish. Red high heels. What should she do with them. She doesn't want the doctors to see.

When he dreams, in the bed where he never awakens, he dreams always that the train is above him. It seems to guard the place in which he sleeps with a bower made of bending metal and electrified third rails. And amidst this, he knows what he is. A legless man. A man surfacing to the slatted windows through which he watched his entire family, separately, eating, undressing, turning away. He thinks, was it a fall or was it a jump and it seems to him that it was a gradual descent. Like the ladder of the tracks reached up toward him and he climbed over the edge ever so gracefully, down toward the bottom where the rats ran rapidly across the tracks. Crossing and crossing and crossing again. And there is a delirium to this, as he feels himself again kicking out against the track, kicking free, and surfacing. And he thinks, if he had only jumped up and clung to the body of the train, he could have stopped it; or it could have carried him like a mother might, with that force and unthinking presumption that renders one's body powerless, through the tracks and tunnels and into the next room where it would put him to bed and perhaps read to him from metal pages, with metal words, about a young boy placed in the way of unwitting disasters, of enchantments, abductions. Of tests that need to be passed over and over and over again.

His wife walks barefoot out of the hospital, holding the shoes out beside her like they are filthy tainted things. Thinking only that she must find a place to hide them. Somewhere at home. Away from the hospital. But when she reaches out to hail a cab, she discovers that her arms will not move. Staying firmly at her sides as if they have formed a strange solidarity with her body. And instead she finds herself walking into the subway tunnel, the vertigo of the train pulling her closer to the tracks. Until she reaches out and touches the door, the window, the corrugated side. The painful feeling as her hand bends back from the speed of the car, one finger settling strangely outside of its socket.

In the train bed, in the bedroom with locomotive wallpaper, his mother reads him stories in a voice that is simultaneously rushed and hushed—moving steadily forward, never stopping long enough to notice him. The force of her. And beneath it he is always small. His questions stolen by the strength of her words, until he stops opening his mouth altogether—afraid that if he does, she will take all that is left of him. Leave him mute. Like boys in stories, exiled to foreign lands, placed in rooms with deadly serpents, robbed of everything that is rightfully theirs. Royalty dethroned. And there are boys burnt by fires before they even grow into men, blinded, sent into the woods to be lost, turned into toads, asses, halves of men, and he wants to ask, how can this be? And he wants to ask, aren't they men of power, aren't they princes? But his mother's voice rolls over his questions so surely that it is as if they have never been spoken.

He waits for wizards, for conjuring men, for anyone who can break the enchantment. But in her tales it is always princesses, sisters, pulling brothers from ovens, from wells in which, transformed, their only power is that of speech. And he thinks, even when they are rescued, they must feel this, mustn't they, the continual sensation of a body torn. And the embrace always somehow harsher than it should be. His dreams full of metal and track, in the bower of the train bed.

And if it was a fall or a jump, it might just as well have been a slow bending at the knee, as if to stoop inconspicuously and pick something from the ground—a penny dropped in the tunnel, a penny placed across the tracks to see what the wheels will do to it. The violence of bent copper, the way the head stretched, stretched flat, stretched again until it grew unrecognizable.

Shoulders tight, his wife tries not to vomit—the doctors telling her how they tried to reattach the legs, tried to stitch arteries and flesh together and failed. They say—there was just too much trauma. The tissue damage was enormous. And while they are talking to her, while they are saying this, she can only think, what have they done with his legs. And she looks behind their backs where their hands are clasped, suspiciously. And looks at her own knees with revulsion. These men should be covered in blood, she thinks. Should come to me holding his legs and say here, these are yours, these belong to you now. Their hands have been somewhere inside him, somewhere she has never imagined touching before, and it is an infidelity. A betrayal. Being told by them only the final of many indignities. And she wishes that she was the one to find him, to lay him carefully out across the kitchen floor and take out her sewing kit, delicately, like darning, her sure stitches. She thinks, I would have found a way to do it. Knows that she would have held the muscle and vein tightly in her hands and simply begun to stitch.

But in the room in which they are hiding half of his body from her, the ends of his bandages are florid red like magician's flowers pulled too quickly from a pocket. And she thinks again that this is a trick. All of it. This presentation of him some elaborate hoax. And she curves herself around him so that her knees touch the bandaged ends and her legs are suddenly his. Furious, she thinks, hermaphrodite. And begins to weep.

When the gulls are after him, as they often are, their shrill voices, the noise of them, he can only think to wave them away with a quick movement of the hand that he hopes will make them disappear. Knowing there must be gestures to ward away such things. Signs and spells and words spoken that he should have been taught.

He remembers the way his briefcase burst open and the papers scattered forth like small white birds from a box, rushing away from him, from the force of the train bearing down upon them. And he thinks what a wonderful gesture that was. The crowd gathering round to see the miraculous performance—a man kneeling in the tracks in a position of prayer, throwing birds out into the tunnel. The bright burst of wings and startled shouts of surprise. The impact of applause so unexpectedly powerful. Bowing down beneath it. Metal hands clapping one against the other. And then the gulls again, tearing at him, his body pressed against the tracks. And he thinks, wasn't there a story told to him, of a man eaten alive by eagles.

Each night his wife sits by the bedside and waits for him to awake, to turn to her, to open his eyes and bring into view so subtly, so miraculously, his real body. To produce from those lividly bandaged bouquets the flowers of his legs for her and to unfurl them like a scarf of bruised-blues. The rotten-appled greens which she sees under the doctor's fingernails, under her own when she touches him. Infected, festering. These fake legs. The blush of bandages. And sometimes she moves toward him and makes the motion of tearing, as if she would remove it all from eyesight. Make it cleaner somehow, more precise. No longer bloodied stumps. This husband whose gown she is afraid to look beneath.

What makes the trick so maddening, she thinks, is the way the toes wiggle at the bottom of the broken box and the head at the other and this trick somehow always angering, she thinks, unamazed. When the saw goes through, and the body, like some sort of garish unwanted gift, remains, there is a feeling of being cheated somehow. And one is obliged to ask—how is this done, doctor, what is the special trick? The deteriorated parlor magic that only little boys perform.

Turbaned, sequined, made up in their mother's thick white paste and shadow, the red bloom of their mouths, their livid cheeks. So intent on amazing. And she curls around his body on the bed and joins her knees to the absence of his once more—as if to assure herself there is no art here. But when she stares at him, out of the corner of her eyes, it is always shyly and with a look of awe, as if expecting, in the end, the boxed bed to open, and something beyond expectation to be revealed. As if she still expects to be amazed after all.

He believes that he should be able to stop it. Or barring that, to bend the tracks so that the rush of train above leaves him untouched. Like he has seen in comic strips, in books read again and again when his mother was not home. Tales of ordinary men made mighty. Of superpowers, of hulks, of supermen. Waiting for the thick bridge of track to bend under his hands.

There was something about a trail. He remembers this. And birds that ate the breadcrumbs that were supposed to lead to safety. Something about his briefcase and a path up out of the tracks. A ladder perhaps. Something he just had time to see as he fell, out of the corners of his eyes. Papers bursting forth. A lock sprung open. And the thought of escape gone the second he saw the train. The tracks like an oven. The heat of them like something from his mother's story. A little boy to be eaten. A hungry witch. And his mother says, you were so stupid, you crawled right inside it. And he thinks, was it a crawl or was it a jump, and he thinks it was a gradual descent. The tracks burning his hands, his thighs, the sensation of unbearable heat and pain as he is pressed against the welts of the tracks. And someone is supposed to open the oven, he thinks. To let him out. Was it a sister?Or maybe a wife.

Waiting, watching him always for the smallest sleight of hand, she wonders whether he needs a turban, a cape, a cane. She twists her scarf around his head, draping a robe over his hospital gown, rouging his face like all good boys who play Houdini. And for a moment she thinks how pretty he could be—pulling the gown down to cover the stumps as best she can before she props the red shoes up against them. So that for a moment he looks whole. Foreshortened like a child. Or a damsel bound to the train tracks who no one has thought to rescue. She thinks, hermaphrodite. And the thought is one which comforts and dismays—her hand hovering above his gown, hesitating to lift it, to discover what sex he has become.

And in the hospital, now devoid of men—a night shift of nurses and insomniac wives—she wonders how it is possible. This story she has been told. This tale. Of another man's hands touching his back for a moment, as quick as a pat on the back, but a push. And he, unable to withstand it, fallen into the train like a child shoved on the playing field. Dropped into an instant position of prayer. Gangly knees always bruised, now broken, severed, shattered under wheels. And she thinks, isn't she supposed to wake him. The taste of metal in her mouth.

all of us are cars
      or, all of us are ears
            (Yankelevich, page 149)

Stopping in Artesia

William Wenthe

How many nights will you be staying?
—Motel Clerk

Out here you can tell a man's work
by his truck. But you're not driving a truck
past gas fields where the sulphur stinks
enough to make you renounce all lungs.
West wind saves this town, agitates among
junipers rooted in sand, each one holding
a shadow deep in its craw. Nobody
loves them, but at least they're good
at staying; not like oil, not like the price
of natural gas. The workday starts early, builds
to a big lunch. In the café, anyone can smoke
if they want to, and most want to. Do you know
the word *gas* comes from *chaos*? And the fire
that cooked your burger came from beneath your feet?
Afternoons are the hard stretch; the sun
the only thing beyond question. It cuts
a white acetylene blaze around the edge
of drawn curtains in your motel room,
while the swamp cooler rattles on the roof;
the road a diesel throb. Remember the junipers
will hold that shadow till nights come
moonless, and shadow swallows all.

Better Lucky Than Good

Peter Nolan Smith

THE COLUMBUS DAY WEEKEND BEGAN WITH A GRIZZLY RAIN splattering on the Hudson. I shut the windows for the first time in months and dressed in heavy clothes for breakfast. The shoes and jacket were unnaturally heavy after a season of shorts and sandals. Luckily global warming guaranteed that the city would heat up before the leaves fell from the trees.

I ran from my apartment building, dodging the raindrops on East Tenth Street. Halfway onto Ninth Street a young man and woman walked my way underneath an umbrella. The long black raincoat acted as a *chador* and a scarf covered pale blonde hair. The hyena laugh betrayed the woman's identity. I almost said hello, but Gabrielle appeared happy and I lowered my head.

She must have recognized my walk, for she called my name with a touch of disbelief.

I feigned surprise. "Gabrielle, I'm surprised to see you in New York."

"I'm shooting a film here, so it's nice to be out of Paris." She tugged the scarf and unleashed her casually coiffed hair. Her beauty remained as intoxicating as our goodbye kiss in Paris. "You haven't aged a day."

"Most men say that." The timeworn compliment was lead to her ears.

"It's the truth." I had seen her in a film by Claude Lelouch the other night. She had been naked. Her breasts lay flat against her chest.

Her blonde hair hung down her back. It was too familiar to view the film's entirety.

"Thanks." She introduced the handsome young man as the lead actor in the movie. "He'll hit it big."

"Only if the camera lets me." His agent must have promised him a golden career.

"Congratulations," I offered, and the actor started a discourse on acting. I cut him short with a question to Gabrielle. "How long are you in town?"

"Just another week. Maybe we can meet for lunch." She stepped closer to the young man to either reheat his interest or for shelter under the umbrella.

I stuck my hands in my pockets. "I'm at the same number."

"The same apartment?"

When we had been contemplating a life together, she had visited the three narrow rooms of 3E. A loft or a hotel room on the park was more a movie starlet's style. "I've been living there since 1977."

"Except for when you stayed with me?" She lilted her head to the side and a golden curtain slipped across her face.

"And a couple of other places." Gabrielle and I might have spent part of a lifetime with each other instead of less than a half-year. It took me a long time to discover that she gave me months more than her other lovers. Wanting more had been asking too much.

"Your friend, Jeffrey, he introduced us."

"Jeffrey's dead almost seven years and his girls are almost grown." Paris and Manhattan were populated by ghosts of both the living and dead. She touched my hand as a silent apology for our failed romance. "And your friends in Paris bet you would go to an early grave. In fact, I heard you died in a motorcycle accident."

"A truck hit me head-on in Burma and killed me instantly." I lifted my bent left wrist. Gabrielle shook her head. "You're joking?"

"I hit the windshield and flipped to land on a pile of rice and an old woman. She looked in the air for the airplane from which I had fallen."

"You were always lucky."

Her words aged me a hundred years, because they weren't true in love. A slide show of our meeting flickered from my memory. She had been the lead in a movie. I had been cast as a thug. The director asked me to rough her up. They should have used a stunt man. I didn't know what to say other than to ask about her one true love. "How's your pig?"

"He passed away a couple of years ago."

I derived no pleasure from her pig's death. "Sorry, you really loved that pig."

"You had a pig?" The young actor expressed his emotive range like he was auditioning for the role of her lover.

"A little pig." I had bought flowers and she had cooked meals fit for a deposed king. Even the end at the airport had been romantic. The hurt came once I got back to New York. "She considered cats and dogs dirty."

"And pigs are clean?" he chuckled and Gabrielle narrowed her Atlantic green eyes.

I decided to further damage his prospects by quickly adding, "Cleaner than humans. They only wallow in the mud to stay cool. Her pig was toilet-trained."

"So you're a pig-lover." The actor was struggling with his composure. I had him right in my sights. "Why not? They saved my life."

"How?"

"It's a long story and we have to rehearse our lines," Gabrielle said. She had heard the tale a long time ago. She leaned forward to kiss me. I knew better than to let my lips touch hers. I turned my head. The twin pecks on the cheeks were a far cry from making love in the shadows of the Tuilleries. "Still wearing Chanel."

"Some things stay the same." The tolling from the St. Mark's steeple broke the spell of the past and she tucked her arm under his. "Good seeing you. Take care."

"Don't worry about me, I'm indestructible." I walked away, soaked by the rain.

I confused her lust for love. My error had hurt and she was right. None of my friends, enemies, or family had expected me to live into my forties. I had been drowned by a double-overhead wave in Bali, beaten to a pulp with baseball bats on the Lower East Side, and survived an Olds 88 T-boning my VW in front of the Surf Nantasket. The other near-death scrapes were countless. A second sooner or later crossing a street and a car might have crushed me on its fender. A slip in the bath and I drown. Fitness had no influence on survival, especially since I had entrusted my life to luck, which offers little protection against the deadliest assassin of all.

Yourself.

In *The Comedians*, Graham Greene writes, "However great a man's fear of life, suicide remains a courageous act, for he has judged by the laws of averages that to live will be more miserable than death. His sense of mathematics has to be greater than his sense of survival."

I had majored in math during college and gambled in Reno on my twenty-first birthday, yet nothing had prepared me for a sudden lurch toward the brink of self-destruction in 1988.

That summer, my faux-cousin, Olivier Brial, had thrown me the keys to his family's beach home. Carnet-sur-Mer wasn't the Riviera. Only the Riviera was the Riviera, but the Mediterranean was just as blue.

I wrote during the day and ate the evening meal with Oliver's family. The town had no nightlife outside the cafés and by the end of August I had completed a collection of short stories. I thanked the Brials for their hospitality and bid Perpignan farewell, fully confident that my book would conquer Manhattan's literary world. I hitchhiked to Avignon and headed into the Luberon Valley, where my friend, Jeffrey Kime, was renovating an ancient villa on the outskirts of Menerbes.

Summer ends slowly in Provence. Jeffrey's dog barked at my arrival. His wife and kids shouted their warm greetings from the terrace. Lunch was set for ten guests. Another place was set at the long table and Jeffrey introduced me as an "author."

After a long repast of fresh vegetables, succulent fish, and melons accompanied by countless bottles of red wine, I read them a story of swimming naked in the Quincy Quarries. Jeffrey's wife claimed I was the "next big writer." Their friends toasted my upcoming success and I retired to the attic bedroom for a dreamless sleep.

Late-August blessed the ruined towns stretching through the Luberon with delightful weather. The company was smart. We read books. Conversations covered the cares of the world punctuated by wit-whipped laughter. The night sky swirled with the cosmos. I should have been happy, only every morning awoke an increasingly profound despair.

This depression was not the result of a mere hangover. I was inflicted with a disease and I diagnosed its source, peeking out the attic's tiny window. Jeffrey's youngest daughter was holding on to the tail of their golden retriever and relieving herself au naturel. Her mother joyously declared, "Matilda's getting toilet-trained by a dog."

My friends were happily married and their lives were moving toward reachable goals. I hadn't had a girlfriend in years and no one really published stories of arson and stealing cars. My future was a life sentence of solitary confinement and I secluded myself in the attic, asking, "What next?" Lifting my eyes to the sky gave me the answer.

Jeffrey's house rested under an escarpment separating the Luberon from the coast. A dirt trail through the vineyards climbed past a quarry. Centuries of labor had created a three-hundred foot cliff. The sheer white face murmured a single syllable. I soon deciphered their whisper into one word.

"Jump."

Not like David Lee Roth sang on Van Halen's second album.

Simply, "Jump."

Jeffrey sensed my dismay. We had all had friends go crazy, some fatally. He didn't leave me on my own, although his surveillance wavered with the preparations for a Sunday lunch. His wife commanded his company for a shopping trip to Avignon. His kids begged me to come along. I had different plans. "You go without me."

"Will you be here when we return?" Jeffrey opened the door to his Volvo. His wife corralled their two daughters into the rear and said, "Where else can he go?"

"Just for a walk in the beautiful French countryside?" I waved goodbye and as soon as the car disappeared around the curve, I set out for the path skirting the cliff face. I rested atop the hill. To the west the River Rhône shimmered as a silvery snake under the noon sun and the northern horizon wore the broken toothed smile of the snowy Alps. Not a cloud spoiled the sky and fragrant wildflowers scented the wind. It was too beautiful for any more words and I walked toward the edge, determined to excise the word "jump" from my vocabulary.

Only twenty feet from eternity I heard an inhuman snort to my right and a nasal grunt to my left. The underbrush rustled apart for two little pigs. They were unusually hairy, primeval, and cute. I took a single step toward them and they shivered out a squeal. A louder snort trumpeted from behind a rock. I froze in place, as a massive boar with yellow curling tusks and coarse black hair coating her sinewy spine trotted protectively before the piglets. The black pearl eyes glared maternal hatred and the beast methodically scraped the earth with a cloven hoof. Its horrible head lowered to charge in a slather. "Jump" was replaced by "run" and I climbed a wizened tree. The boar rammed the trunk several times. Its babies scooted into the bushes and the ugly brute vanished from the plateau. Not sure it wasn't playing a trick, I swayed in the tree for another minute, exhilarated that my will to survive had overpowered my will to die.

Some priests might have deemed the incident a miracle and I might have offered a prayer in thanks, only I wasn't sure which saint was the patron of pigs. I dropped from the tree and headed to Jeffrey's house.

The kids were chasing each other in a squall of shouts, the guests were drinking rosé and conversing about a nearby neighbor's book about life in Provence. Jeffrey's wife was slicing a slab of meat for the barbecue and my friend was peeling potatoes. Obviously relieved by my reappearance, he asked, "Where have you been?"

"Out for a walk." Explaining my mad dash from suicide was a topic for another day and I helped chop the potatoes with a knife. It was sharp and I was careful. "What are we having for dinner?"

"A nice roasted pork." Jeffrey beamed with a lean hunger.

"Pork?" I protested and Jeffrey scowled, "You convert to Islam?"

"No visions, a change of heart." Grateful to the boar's intercession, if only momentarily, I said, "I'll stick to the potatoes for today."

"Suit yourself," Jeffrey shrugged and I basked idiotically in my triumph over a desperate desire to leave this life before my time. In Paris Jeffrey introduced me to Gabrielle. I was happy for a while. Not forever, but that romance is a story for a day without the sizzle of bacon waffling on the drizzle.

I entered Veselka and the counterman took my order. At fifty, asking for anything more from life than breakfast becomes risky, but I can deal with surprises, because I've had practice, for while pigs can't fly, they sometimes can save your life.

The List

Janet Kaplan

A can of carrots, shipped overnight to headquarters. Without peas. "Seasons greetings, carrots," the detective said. He stepped out for a smoke. The oyster house was for sale, the hardware store, the boatyard, the business that sold "for sale" signs. Even the criminals had gone back to the land. Before escaping, Turtledove made a list of her crimes. Locked doors, broken dolls, faulty DNA. She left the list where the detective would find it. There were dangers in reading such lists but he would be all right. A new kind of surgery was in the works: the heart removed and not replaced. Vessels linked in an endless loop. Oxygen waving like mad as it comes 'round the bend.

Children love dinosaurs because if dinosaurs existed, we would not. (Shapiro, page 209)

Interior, Exterior, Portrait, Still-Life, Landscape

George Rush
Wayne Gonzales
Bill Adams
Sally Ross
Juliana Ellman

Curated by Cameron Martin

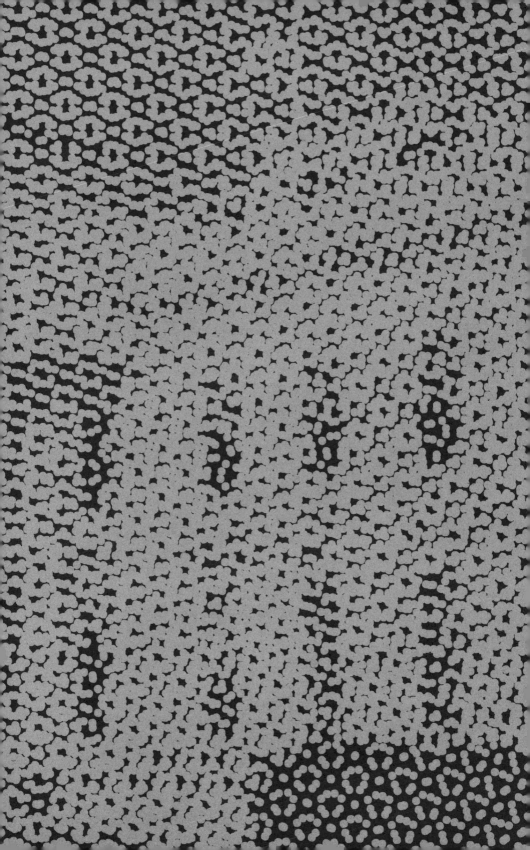

Jack and the Rotarians

Luis Jaramillo

JACK AND THE ROTARIANS WERE NO LONGER SPEAKING. THEY ALL sat in the Masonic hall and ate their chicken and baked potatoes grimly, sawing at the dry flesh out of habit even though they weren't hungry. No one had ever invited a Mexican before.

The Mexican was a doctor and he wasn't actually from Mexico. He came from Los Angeles and he was my father, which is why I'm telling this story.

This story is actually the convergence of two events on one day. Nobody talks about coincidence in Salinas. Nobody runs into anybody and thinks, "What a small world." This is only to say that because it was a small town, of course I knew Jack's son.

Jack Jr. and I ran the mile and two mile for the middle-school track team. Jack Sr. coached the long-distance runners and that night, that same Wednesday, the Wednesday that my father attended the Rotary meeting for the first time and the Wednesday of the track meet, Jack Jr. and I kissed.

Kissing is often the point of the story but in this story it isn't. It is the thing that happened that day, but it isn't the point—the kissing was incidental, only one event. There is a Latin term for the assumption that the first action causes the next, just because the two events follow sequentially. My dad said the phrase all the time as a warning against such thinking, *post hoc ergo propter hoc*, after this means because of this. But he meant the opposite. We were supposed to remember it was a fallacy.

At the track meet that afternoon, it was hard for us seventh graders to know what exactly had happened at the lunch meeting and why it mattered. After the dads dropped their kids off, they stood around together, kicking at the grass with their hands in their pockets. We all overheard them talking, "Next thing you know, it'll be all greasers at the meeting." Or, "It had to happen sometime," and, "His son is on the track team, you know."

None of the fathers spoke to Jack Sr.

Jack Sr. didn't care. As a pre-meet warm-up he practiced his favorite activity. While we ran warm-up laps, he ran around the track ahead of us, juggling three tennis balls. He called this joggling.

"Come on you slugs, I could run faster than you even if these tennis balls were axes."

His antics didn't help me. Everybody knew that I was the child of the Mexican who'd gone to the Rotary Club meeting. My teammates looked at me with a kind of awe. I'd never been Mexican before and now I was.

I lived in a house with a pool and my family took trips. I had one sister. My mother didn't push the shopping cart back from the grocery store with all of her children trailing behind. I'd always been brown, but now I was a Mexican.

Nobody said anything to me that day. Maybe they were afraid that I'd stop being a Mexican and that they would look foolish for thinking I was something I wasn't.

Jack Jr. was thin and tall. He had blond hair and very pale skin. He was built like a long-distance runner. He would have been considered good looking, but he often had a worried look on his face. When it was time to pick on the fat kid, or the nerd, he just watched. He didn't defend anybody but he didn't say anything mean either.

This is the same day, the same story. This isn't the day, two weeks in the future when, at the next meet, Jack Jr. elbowed me in the ribs to get around me on his final kick to the finish line, even though we were on the same team. He threw his bony arm into my side, leaving a bruise, and he didn't apologize afterward.

This isn't the time years later, in high school, that we sat on the bus with our bare legs touching on the way back from Monterey, our heads hunched close to the portable video football game.

This is still the Wednesday of that first Rotary meeting my dad attended with Jack Jr.'s dad.

We wore our singlets and the silky shorts that grazed the tops of our thighs, sweat pants and sweat shirts over the racing wear. We ran in our regular running shoes. Our racing flats, tied together around our necks, bounced on our chests. As a team, we long-distance runners ran wide laps around the playing field, jogging slowly to warm up.

I ran just ahead of Jack Jr.

"Hey," Jack Jr. said, covering his mouth so that his father wouldn't see.

"What?"

"Let's not race today. Let's ditch."

"Okay," I said. I didn't know what we would do or where we would go but it seemed that Jack Jr. had a plan. I didn't think past the moment of escape because it was the escape itself that was thrilling. It was dangerous—I knew we'd be caught—but I liked the idea of hiding. The danger wasn't the attraction, the hiding was. Of course one thing causes another.

We waited until nobody, no adult, was looking. Then we told Jake McInnis and Jeff Wong that we were going to the bathroom. After we made it around the corner, we kept jogging to the bike rack. We unlocked our bikes then climbed on. We pedaled fast.

We rode to Jack Jr.'s grandparent's house. Jack Jr. fished the key out from the birdhouse hanging under the eaves of the front porch. The older Churches had gone down to Cabo San Lucas and we had the house to ourselves.

Jack Jr. showed me a refrigerator in the garage full of Miller Lite. We cracked open beers and sat in lounge chairs on the back deck. The beer tasted like aluminum and it was very cold.

"This beats running around that damn track."

"Yeah. Damn racing."

"Do you want a cigarette?" Jack Jr. motioned me over to his deck chair. He had a pack in the pocket of his sweatpants, as if he smoked all the time. He lit the cigarette with a lighter and blew out the smoke. He waved the pack at me. I took one of the cigarettes and put it in my mouth. He waved the flame of the lighter in front of my cigarette.

"Inhale like your mother just came into the room."

I tried it, gasping in the smoke.

I coughed violently. His trick worked.

"Have you ever kissed a girl?" Jack Jr. asked.

"No, have you?" My eyes watered from the smoke but I kept at it.

"What do you think it's like?"

We got another couple of beers from the garage then sat down next to each other on the same deck chair.

We'd already left the meet, we'd be kicked off the team, and probably suspended too. In the future we wouldn't even live in the same town. I would want to kiss boys and Jack Jr. wouldn't, but that night, that Wednesday, it didn't matter. We were going to do everything bad all at once.

Jack took a film canister out of his backpack and showed me the marijuana inside. He took out rolling papers and tried to look like he knew what he was doing. His hands shook and the paper made a noise like a leaf. He said curse words under his breath.

When he was done, the joint looked wrong. I didn't know exactly what it should have looked like, but I knew it was too fat on one end and it was kind of loose, so the marijuana dribbled out unless Jack tilted it at a crazy angle. Jack lit it and inhaled. It worked even though it was messy.

I inhaled too. We relaxed against the back of the chair.

"Running sucks," I said. I didn't mean it. I liked running, I just didn't like to race.

"Yeah," Jack said. He put his arms over his head. We sat very close together on the deck chair.

Jack leaned over and kissed me, slipping his tongue in my mouth for a second.

I was horrified and I wanted more. I pulled my mouth away.

"It's probably better with a girl," Jack Jr. said.

That was it.

"Let's have another cigarette," I said. I liked how smoking gave me something to do with my hands.

We shared another cigarette. Neither one of us smoked properly. I felt so happy to be smoking badly next to Jack Jr. We weren't even friends.

We drank another beer each and talked about Dungeons and Dragons. We never knew the other also liked to play. We made a plan to play and smoke a joint before we played. I decided I was a stoner.

I'd heard of people getting hooked right off, and I guessed I was one of them.

I'd never had a whole beer to myself before, let alone two. I felt tired and I wanted to close my eyes, so I let them shut. Jack Jr. must have passed out soon after I did.

My father and Jack Sr. found us lying on the one chair. We were so small that we fit, snuggled next to each other like children.

"Let's talk *mi hijo*," my father said, in the car on the way home.

The Miller Lite addled my brain and I thought I might be sick on the floor. Mostly I still felt very tired. I closed my eyes, leaning my head against the glass of the car door.

"I won't do it again," I said. I didn't specify what I meant.

"I know you won't. You are an ethical person."

I pressed more of my face on the cool glass, wishing my dad would stop talking.

"When I was little I used to be able to fly. I flew around the back-yard when nobody was there. But then I got scared that somebody would see me, so I stopped."

"That's not true," I said. The story was meant to make me laugh, but it didn't work. It worried me that it might be true. Even then I knew that he was talking about something sexual because the flying was shameful. Something shameful is probably true and this is what worried me. I didn't want my dad to fly.

Later, I pieced together a more complete picture of that day. Jack Sr. had started up a campaign to get my father into the Rotary Club. Step one was to get him to the meeting. He pursued my father like a lover. He called my father every day, "Why don't you want to come to the meeting? It won't hurt you. It'll be good for the community. If you come, I'll teach you how to juggle."

Years before the meeting, Jack Sr. had gone away to college, then came back to this small farming town to go into his father's line of business, insurance. He sold insurance to farmers and lawyers and doctors and made plenty of money at it. The Churches were an old family, old for California, and people trusted them. The Churches might be wild as youngsters—get drunk and flip a car or grow long hair—then they always settled into the family business.

But something happened to Jack Sr. at college. Lots of people pick up a veneer of liberalism, but most of us are lazy. We aren't willing to make our vision real. Jack Sr. saw how the town he came from functioned, and decided to do something about it. He came back to the town with plans. My father was one of Jack Sr.'s projects.

After months of phone calls, my father gave in.

"I'll go to the meeting."

At the meeting that Wednesday, Jack introduced my father around. During the luncheon, the man sitting next to my father, one of the bank vice presidents, leaned over and said, "You speak English good for a Mexican."

My father said, "Thank you. You speak well yourself."

The man looked pleased, but unsure whether or not he'd been insulted. It didn't matter. An insult from a Mexican only meant the Mexican was looking for trouble.

Jack Sr. and my father became friends. The racist old bastards either died or gave up, and Jack stuck around, my father stuck around.

My dad joined Rotary and attended meetings every week, no matter where he was, even when vacationing in Thailand or in Sun Valley for the the annual cardiologists convention. When he was in town, my dad sat next to Jack. Those two never stopped planning or making things happen in the town.

At the last Rotary meeting, the last Wednesday of this story, my father urged Jack to eat the cherry pie served to him even though it wasn't very good.

"You only live once. Waste not want not." And my dad meant both things. He actually knew about wanting.

My father was too intelligent—he was a doctor, after all—to blame himself when the next day Jack clutched his chest and fell to the floor, dead.

Jack was still young. The Churches didn't die young. Everybody came to the funeral.

Even I came. I took an airplane and rented a car and I came home.

At the reception, I saw Jack Jr. standing in a line with the rest of his family, shaking hands. We'd lost touch. He looked like his father. He had the same energy around him, like a suit. Jack Jr. was a little thicker in the middle but still tall, of course, and he was deeply tanned, crows feet around his eyes.

My father whispered to me that Jack Jr. was a doctor now too. He had a wife and a baby girl. He had a clinic and didn't charge people who couldn't pay. My father had told me this before, but I let him tell me again.

Jack Jr. smiled when he saw me. He broke out of the receiving line, "I'm glad you came." He put out his arms to be hugged.

"Your father was a good man. He'll be missed." I said. I felt Jack Jr. shaking like he was crying. He wasn't. He couldn't stop laughing. Maybe we both remembered the same things. Jack laughed so much, tears ran down his face.

"I know," he said. "I loved him so much." We clutched each other like men.

Did I mention my father? He lives way down the lake. I want everything to be the way it was before I left. (Raffel, page 181)

The Diagnosis

Daniel John

her mother flew heavily down
from Philadelphia

to drip pity
all over her daughter

and her daughter's pancreas
that cantankerous old man of a boulder

three years later cancer is thrilled
to still be alive

but everybody else
is stone-cold exhausted

death in particular
is so crowded

he can hardly
breathe

The next song was about
a chocolate box from Paris full of love,
which was nice too, but as summer burned on then burned
its oily clunker of a motor out, the songs began sounding
all the same, only a little different, like the same
(Knox, page 129)

Number One Tuna

Amber Dermont

MALCOLM AND I ONLY STAYED IN TOUCH BECAUSE WE WERE EACH privately convinced that the other deserved to fail. We'd been roommates at Haverford, Malcolm's first choice, my safety. Since neither one of us really cared for the other, we decided to live together for all four years. "Friends," we assured each other, "make bad roommates." Around campus we appeared cordial, but inside our dorm room we cultivated an exquisite wall of contempt. I just barely tolerated the jizzed condom trophies Malcolm hid under his bed, the skid marks he left on the boxers he borrowed from me, and his insistent declaration that he had J. Crew looks. In turn, Malcolm endured my noisy, bubbling fish tank, my mother's late night phone calls, and my pathological habit of quoting from *All About Eve*. "Fasten your seat belts; it's going to be a bumpy night!" I'd exclaim every time he brought over a girl from Bryn Mawr.

After college, we both relocated to Los Angeles. Malcolm used connections I never knew he had and finagled a studio job. An uncle of mine wheedled me an assistant-to-a-paralegal position at a law office in Brentwood. Malcolm and I had stopped living together at this point, but we kept in touch. Once a month, Malcolm destroyed my tennis confidence, then later made nice by taking me out to a new sushi palace. I was mostly friendless in L.A., and I kept hoping that Malcolm might invite me to a glitzy premiere, introduce me to a horny starlet, or better still, arrange a job interview for me at Paramount. Then the worst thing in the world happened. Malcolm sold a screenplay.

He grossed $100,000 for the first one. I comforted myself by doing the math: the taxes he paid, his agent's cut. I figured Malcolm took home $35,000. I could live with that. It wasn't much more than what I made in a year. It never occurred to me that his film would be produced. The film, of course, earned seven Oscar nominations. While it lost Best Picture to that movie about the glow-in-the-dark children and the nuclear winter, Malcolm himself won for Best Original Screenplay. Three minutes after his victory speech, his agent unloaded his second screenplay for a million dollars. In quick succession, Malcolm had a development deal, a production company, and a 20,000 gallon aquarium filled with baby sharks he'd netted in Fiji.

The party invitation simply stated: "Welcome the Stingray." Malcolm lived in a glass mansion high in the Hollywood Hills. As I drove up the narrow curving road, I marveled at the hazy view that stretched from downtown all the way to the beach and out further to the pounding and polluted Pacific surf. His house, while not enormous, was exceptional. The front entryway boasted a soaring glass atrium. With a push of a button, Malcolm could frost the clear glass, tint it blue, or drop steel curtains down on every wall.

Malcolm had hired the requisite valets to park cars outside his glass mansion. The car jockeys were on a cigarette break when I pulled up in my Ford Festiva. Knowing that the valets would finish every last drag before coming to my aid, I climbed out of the car and lit up a Camel. One of the valets moved close enough to fling a plastic ticket at me. He motioned for my keys. I tossed my key chain at him then finished my cigarette, slowly. I'd spent two hours in traffic driving from Tarzana. I was in no hurry.

I'd never been to a party for a fish before. At a loss for what to wear, I'd cruised the vintage stores on Melrose and purchased a blue and white striped seersucker suit. The waifish shopgirl used the words "dapper" and "jazz age" as I modeled outside the dressing room. I quoted the last line of *The Great Gatsby* as she swiped my debit card: "So we beat on, boats against the current, borne back ceaselessly into the past." She said something about the scene in the book where Mia Farrow fondles all of Robert Redford's dress shirts. For a moment, I actually considered inviting her to the party. I'd been dateless for months, but Malcolm would have sneered at the waif's narrow hips and flat chest and asked me, "Where do you keep her tits?" As I made my solitary stroll to Malcolm's glass house, the dark lights on the pathway brightened, glowed, and dimmed as I passed them.

The stingray was Malcolm's new pet and his newest pet project, the title of his latest screenplay, an intellectual action film, with a marine biologist/chemical weapons expert for a hero. The film would mark Malcolm's directorial debut. He'd bought himself a giant fish to celebrate the studio green-lighting the project. He already owned a Corvette Stingray with a vanity plate that read, "STUNG."

Dazzling female bodies wrapped in gauzy gowns and male bodies covered in colorful, collarless shirts pushed and pulled in small schools inside the foyer's atrium. The centerpiece of the room was an octagonal aquarium, approximately eight feet tall, with thick glass walls, and an open top. Five adolescent sharks, a giant sea turtle, and an enormous winged stingray patrolled the waters. I watched the stingray flutter and float above the sharks' bodies. The stingray, silvery and menacing on top, had a creamy pink bottom. As the ray flashed its belly against the glass, I saw its mouth arched in a perfect smile. The perma-grin on his underside gave the stingray a comic, strangely human quality. When I left Haverford for L.A., I gave up my own gurgling fish tanks. Flushed my collection of hatchet fish, triggerfish, and tailbar lionfish. I had no one to give them to, no way to keep them.

I spotted our host's bald head. He'd shaved his scalp for the Academy Awards, and now kept his head tanned and polished. In college, Malcolm wore his hair in a blond afro. I had to admit that his big, shiny noggin looked, in a certain light, like a polished Etruscan phallus. Like Yul Brunner in *The King and I*, Malcolm commanded authority. Bareheaded with bare feet, outfitted from head to ankle in white linen, he kept the party spinning around him. A leather cord lassoed around his neck was punctuated by a broken piece of shell. I used to wear a necklace like that my freshman year in college until Malcolm told me the Bryn Mawr girls were questioning my sexual orientation. The woman hanging on Malcolm's arm wore an orange sheath dress. Large gold earrings complimented her tawny skin. This woman didn't seem to be aware that there was a party going on. Before I could interrupt and say hello, she turned to Malcolm and let loose her husky voice, "I'm going to love you like nobody's loved you, come rain or come shine."

Malcolm held the woman's shoulders as she sang. Her voice was otherworldly. Smitten guests paused their own chatter. I heard someone whisper, "That's Quincy Jones's daughter." I couldn't remember who Quincy Jones was, but I knew he was someone important. When she finished, Malcolm took her by the hand, spun her around, and pulled her into his chest. I needed a drink.

The bartender was a redhead named Desi. "Like Desi Arnaz?" I said. She frowned at me. "Short for Desire," she said. The catering company had dolled her up in a blue and green batiked sarong. I wanted to rub her bare shoulders and count the freckles on her back. Instead, I asked for a gin and tonic, and stared down at the uneven cuffs on my new, vintage trousers. I kept going to Malcolm's parties because he kept inviting me. He kept inviting me out of guilt.

The screenplay that Malcolm won an Oscar for was based on a series of telephone conversations he had with my mother during our sophomore year. That year, I'd scored a job as a projectionist for the Bette Davis Film Festival. The first night we screened a double feature: *A Stolen Life* followed by *Of Human Bondage*. Bette Davis was magnificent in *A Stolen Life*. She played twin sisters who fall in love with a lighthouse inspector in Martha's Vineyard. The bad twin wins Glenn Ford's heart, only to die in a boating accident. The good twin must decide whether to pose as her bad twin in order to reclaim Glenn Ford's love. When I got back to our dorm room, I discovered Malcolm on the phone with my mother. He was taking notes.

Malcolm's first screenplay opens with full-frontal nudity, a shot of a young man running naked through the snow. In the background, the audience hears gunfire, barking dogs, men cursing loudly in Russian. We witness the man being captured, being forced to dig his own grave. Then we flash forward to a shot of this same man, decades older, dressed in a gabardine business suit, dining at the Four Seasons in Manhattan. The man in question was my maternal grandfather, Vadim Kaminsky. A minor Soviet dissident who claimed to have once played chess with Trotsky, he then survived the Holocaust, escaped from the gulag, and rose to fame in the United States as an accomplished neurosurgeon. I'd heard the story numerous times. It never occurred to me that my grandfather's life was sufficiently cinematic.

My grandfather hadn't been buried alive, merely threatened. Malcolm had my mother's full permission to write anything he wanted. He never actually met my grandfather until after the script sold. My grandfather was a muscular man, and rambunctious. A fierce hand-shaker. He appeared with Malcolm on *The Charlie Rose Show*, the *Today Show*, and *E! News Live*. He made a special appearance at *The Golden Globe Awards* with John Malkovich, his older screen-self. Malcolm made my grandfather happier than I'd ever seen him. When my grandfather died three weeks before the Academy ballots were due, I knew that Malcolm would win one of those gold, bald statues.

I hadn't expected to see my mother at Malcolm's party, but there she was, wearing a killer Armani suit. Flaunting cleavage. My mother had been a Philadelphia housewife and high school substitute history teacher until Malcolm fixed her up as a consultant for his production company. She had a condo in Santa Monica and a cottage in Palm Springs. I watched from a distance as she hugged Malcolm. My mother rubbed her lipstick off his cheek. My grandfather had been married six times—one of the facts left out of the film version, where he falls in love with Björk at the Black Sea in 1931, and marries her in Brighton Beach in 1950. The man had a stable of children. Even though he was wealthy, he kept forgetting my mother was one of his daughters. She never really had money until Malcolm. My mother had offered to ask Malcolm to get me a consulting position as well, but I'd just been pro-moted to full-fledged paralegal, so I had to turn her down.

My mother pointed out a yellow stain on the right lapel of my suit, and asked if I'd heard anything from my father.

"He got your last check."

"Tell him he should come out and visit." My mother took a sip from my gin and tonic, leaving the rest of her lipstick on my glass.

"That's one hell of a stingray," I said.

"Did you bring anyone?" she asked. "I've been seeing a golf pro."

My mother not only looked young, she looked better than me. I wanted to tell her that she was radiant, that California was good for her, that my father, a hapless actuary, had never appreciated her. I wanted to ask her out to lunch, and I wanted to pay for the meal.

"How's the new film?" I smiled. "Are you and Malcolm working your magic?"

Mom described an action sequence involving a dozen scuba divers, a fleet of jet skis, and a pair of manatees. I half-listened, thinking instead about what kind of mother she'd been and what kind of son I was. When I was ten, I gave her a black lacquer music box for Mother's Day. It was the only gift I could remember giving her. Every time my parents fought, I'd sneak into their bedroom, find the music box and play it. I'd crank the key and hear "Beautiful Dreamer." The inside of the box was lined with red felt. When I lifted the lid, a small plastic man and an even smaller plastic woman popped up on a tiny plastic post. The man and woman held each other, pirouetting to the music. I'd watch the dancers and imagine my mother and father as Ginger Rogers and Fred Astaire in *Top Hat*, Judy Garland and Fred Astaire in *Easter Parade*, Leslie Caron and Fred Astaire in *Daddy Long Legs*, Cyd Charisse and Fred Astaire in *Silk Stockings*. Mom caught me with the box twice. The first time she asked me if I wanted dancing lessons. The second time she checked her underwear drawer, counted her high heels, and asked me if there was anything special I wanted to tell her.

Mom was still gushing about Malcolm, calling him an auteur and promising that *The Stingray* would revolutionize filmmaking. I held up a cigarette and said, "Sorry, Mom, I need a smoke."

As I passed through the crush of guests, I felt a hand on my arm. I turned around and saw Malcolm's shining head.

"You're maudlin and full of self-pity," he said. "You're magnificent."

"What are you talking about?" I asked.

"*All About Eve*. You were always quoting it in college. I finally saw it the other day. It's a little long, but worth remaking."

I said, "I can see your career rise in the East like the sun."

"Excuse me?"

"Another line," I said. "From the same movie."

"I'm thinking of remaking it," he said. "Updating it. Make the ladies movie stars instead of stage actresses. I'm thinking Sharon Stone and that girl from *American Beauty*. It's time to revive their careers."

"Bette Davis will find you and kill you." I tossed an unlit cigarette into my mouth.

"The original won six Oscars." Malcolm pulled the cigarette from my lips and put it behind his ear. "I figure I can win ten."

I snatched my cigarette back. "Promise me you won't remake it."

"I've been thinking you should go to law school," Malcolm gave me a smile and a wink. "I mean, legally, how long can you stay a paralegal?"

"Don't worry about me. I'll surprise you yet."

Malcolm grinned. "Your mom says you're coveting my life. Are you?" A claw of admirers closed in around him before I had a chance to choose my answer.

The back courtyard was landscaped with a koi pond, fruit trees, and a narrow lap pool with special jets that re-created stressful water currents. I needed a cigarette, but my lighter wouldn't work. A woman standing under a lemon tree held a lit cigarette in one hand and a blistered yellow fruit in the other. She dragged on the cigarette, exhaled, brought the lemon to her face, inhaled. She saw me notice her and said, "I'm testing out my senses."

This woman had the tiniest waist I'd ever seen. She also had lustrous brown hair, large round eyes, a long and delicate neck. Audrey Hepburn, only not in a cultivated don't-I-look-like-Audrey-Hepburn way. As she smoked, she hummed, "I Wanna Be Sedated," by the Ramones. When I asked her for a light, she stopped humming and smiled. "Don't you hate L.A. Don't you hate that no one smokes. That no one smokes the way they did in the old movies."

We chatted about smoker's guilt, about sneaking butts in our offices. "I'll take two puffs, tamp the cigarette out, and seal it in an envelope for later. I have dozens of cigarette envelopes waiting for me in my file cabinet," Audrey Hepburn admitted. We debated nicotine gum versus the patch versus hypnosis. Placed bets on our lung cancer odds. She pouted. Blew smoke rings.

"What I really hate about L.A. are actors who know nothing about films," I said.

"All of these bombshells and boneheads want to be stars, yet none of them have ever seen a real movie," she said, rolling the lemon in her palm. "Not *Whatever Happened to Baby Jane?* or *Roman Holiday* or *Badlands*. Not even *Klute*. At best, they cried during *Schindler's List* or sniffled through *Terms of Endearment*."

"Have you ever noticed that no one in L.A. owns any books?" I asked.

"Why would you, when the mansions don't have bookshelves? People don't even pretend to read."

We introduced ourselves. Her name was Naomi and she worked at Fang & Moon, a talent management agency. I'd interviewed there for a position less than a year ago. I'd been called back twice, and I was really hopeful, but the job had gone to someone with an MBA and a J.D. Naomi was the kind of woman I'd look forward to seeing at work every day. After years in L.A., I was stunned to finally meet the girl I'd most likely been looking for. As a child, I loved musicals. I thought being happy meant breaking out into song and tap dancing. I imagined serenading Naomi with "S'wonderful, S'marvelous, you should care for me." I'd pull her in close and we'd twirl and splash in Malcolm's koi pond. Like we were Audrey Hepburn and Fred Astaire in *Funny Face*. Pretending that we, too, were magical.

When Naomi introduced me to her boyfriend Clay, I had a hard time focusing on his face. Clay had blond, sculpted hair. My hand disappeared into his paw as we shook our greetings. Naomi explained to me that she and Clay worked together. Clay had joined the agency less than a year ago.

"Are you talent or production?" Clay asked me.

I hesitated. "I'm behind the scenes."

As Clay wrapped his arms around Naomi and kissed her long, delicate neck, I realized that this guy had my job and my girlfriend. It was one thing to be jealous of Malcolm—I knew I couldn't compete with his fame or his level of success—but my envy of Clay was unacceptable.

Yukio, Malcolm's private chef, accosted me outside the first floor bathroom. He wanted to know if I thought Malcolm looked healthier now than he had at Haverford. Yukio was at the party as a friend, not in any professional capacity. I said that I thought Malcolm looked healthy, but that he'd confided in me earlier that he kept finding blood in his stool. "Don't mention it to him," I said. "He's very sensitive."

"Does he have colon cancer?" Yukio asked.

"You didn't hear it from me."

Yukio promised that he wouldn't betray my confidence. "It might be the mercury in his diet. Malcolm loves fish: swordfish, yellowfin, eel."

I told Yukio that I was especially fond of yellowfin tuna. "I might well be one of the foremost L.A. sushi connoisseurs," I said.

"You've never actually tasted real yellowfin." Yukio laughed. "In order to get real number one tuna, you need to know someone in Chile, a fish boss who can set aside steaks from the Japanese sushi mafia. You, friend, have no idea how good it really is."

As I stalked the party, double-fisting gin and tonics, I heard snippets of conversation.

"It's all about stripping away artifice."

"Who's your blood donor?"

"The Dalai Lama really cracks me up."

"All I want to do is find something fourteen-year-old boys want, and sell it to them."

"He's not just my ex-husband, he's my best friend."

"Is she still eating? I thought she'd stopped."

Malcolm kept a white grand piano in the atrium. I sat down at the piano bench. As I stared at the keys, I thought about what I might play, if I knew how to play the piano. The theme from *Doctor Zhivago*, the theme from *Ice Castles*. A skinny guy in a purple and white striped seersucker suit stood next to the bench. His suit was tailored and the seersucker looked fine and crisp, as though it had been made from something other than seersucker. I recognized him from the movie. He'd played my grandfather as a teenager.

"Aren't you somebody?" he asked me.

"Afraid not." I smiled.

"Everyone kept telling me that there was someone else here wearing a suit like mine. I was hoping for a fashion cat fight."

"Sorry if I'm not perpetuating the Hollywood myth for you."

"At least you're gay," my young grandfather said. "Malcolm always promises me beautiful boys. Never delivers."

"I'm not particularly gay," I said.

"Well, lucky for you, I'm not particular. Do you play piano?" He sat down next to me and played the opening to "Moon River." A wave of guests surged toward the piano player. Malcolm's tawny chanteuse began to sing. I found myself pushed off the bench.

One of the catering waiters stood on a stepladder and tossed platters of frozen meats into the aquarium. The sharks swam to the top of the tank, the high water churning purple. I counted four small-sized sharks, each one dark gray with black spots. Their rows of teeth flashed white as they dined. I hummed the theme from *Jaws*. The sea turtle swam to the bottom of the tank, avoiding the feeding frenzy. The stingray made his rounds in the middle of the pool. When his tray was empty, the waiter climbed down from the ladder and left.

I suspected that the sharks did not get enough to eat. The stingray's wings were stained with blood from the frozen meat. When the first shark nipped the stingray, I was surprised that his teeth left almost no impression. The second shark bit the stingray's tail. I pounded on the glass, "Stop it. That's not fair." All four sharks made passes, attacking the stingray. I climbed up onto the ladder, stared down at the blurry fake ocean, and jumped into the tank.

I couldn't see much underwater. The sharks were silver shadows. As I tried kicking at their heads, my loafers fell off. I dove down and searched for the stingray, eventually grabbing hold of his tail. I pulled the stingray close to my chest and swam to the top of the tank. The fish did not sting me. When I broke the surface, I balanced the ray against the edge of the tank, pulled myself up onto the ladder, and carried the injured fish down to the marble floor. The skin felt slippery and cold. Bitten and bloody, the stingray was still smiling its perma-grin.

While it's true that almost everyone would like to make a movie, only a few people know what that film would be. Some know the title. Others have pre-picked the soundtrack. They've fantasized about casting Drew Barrymore against type or making Steve Buscemi the romantic lead. Only a small percentage of people know how their film would begin, and only I would start with a tracking shot of a man driving a Ford Festiva through the Hollywood Hills. Hardly anyone knows how their film would end, but most would want their ending to be happy.

Soaking wet, I carried the stingray out to Malcolm's backyard and dumped the bloody fish into his koi pond. A crowd of guests was gathering around me. I heard Yukio chiding me for putting a saltwater fish into fresh water. The actor who played my young grandfather joking about stingray sushi. My mother saying, "How embarrassing," and telling me that I would catch pneumonia. Malcolm walked up to me. I saw him smiling sadly.

"You're a good guy," he said. "But face it. The stingray's dying. It's about to die. What were you trying to cast yourself as? Comic relief?"

"No," I replied. "I'm the hero."

Some of the guests began to snicker. Malcolm walked back toward his glass house. The crowd began to thin. I stepped into the pond and saw the stingray lying on its back, smiling up at me. I overheard Naomi saying to Quincy Jones's daughter, "I met him earlier, but I didn't catch his name."

One of the first spring days, when all the people are into this big phony smiley culture everywhere you go—pastel and white and Ray-Bans and automatic cameras in Providence, for Christ's sake— (Douglas, page 151)

To Weldon Kees

Matthew Fluharty

Don't tell me Dwight Eisenhower had the heart of a cabbage.

Don't tell me the same doctor that delivers the babies orders the hearse.

Don't tell me about the canonized underworld of San Francisco Bay.

Don't tell me it's all call and response in this gray divide.

Don't tell me you actually made it to Mexico and will never read this poem.

Don't tell me about love, about a good chord on a bad piano.

Don't tell me we're destined to suffer like Bud Powell and Buddy Bolden,
    running our fingers along the ledge.

Don't tell me all the loneliness and cold radiators.

Don't tell me about AM radio's holy recriminations, american poetry's
    dead headlight.

Don't tell me you tried to hollow out a space in heaven with the blunt
    end of a jackhammer.

Don't tell me an almanac of loss exists on a farther coast, just beyond
    our reach

"There's something about Oliver Stone movies. They radiate sexiness. They radiate sexiness. With Jim Morrison it's easy, because he's so fucking sexy, but even something like Platoon has erotic qualities." (Charles, page 41)

The Grant

Alicia Erian

ROSALIE WASN'T SURE WHAT TO DO ABOUT BIBBS. HE WASN'T very flexible. They had a long-distance relationship going, but whenever Rosalie drove up to Orono, Bibbs wouldn't stop working. All of Rosalie's friends in New York said this was wrong. They said that since Bibbs made his own hours—which he did, he was on sabbatical from the University of Maine, working on a book about voter turnout in New England—he could surely make up whatever time he'd lost after Rosalie left. When Rosalie suggested this to Bibbs, however, he became enraged. "What if I was a dentist?" he yelled. "Would you have me stay home from work then?" Rosalie asked, "But you're not a dentist," and Bibbs shook his head and said he knew she would say that.

After a few months of this, Rosalie broke up with Bibbs in her mind. She just hadn't told Bibbs yet. She didn't really want to break up with him, was the thing. When Bibbs wasn't running their relationship to his specifications, Rosalie really liked him. What was worse, she even liked him when he was running the relationship. Not in a normal way, she knew, but it still felt like liking.

Bibbs's specifications made Rosalie want him to hurt her when they were in bed. Actually, hurt wasn't the right word. It was more that she wanted him to humiliate her. When she woke up in the morning and her mind was a little loose, she imagined things she thought she might like. Maybe when he was fucking her, Bibbs could pin her wrists, Rosalie thought. Or maybe he could tell her to get on her stomach, then fuck her that way, gripping the back of her neck with his hand. Or maybe he could command her at some odd moment to strip and start touching herself.

Just thinking about these things made Rosalie wet. She put a hand between her legs, played with one of her nipples, and said Bibbs's name when she came. He'd told her once that he'd like for her to do this, and she was glad at least for this little bit of instruction.

The next time Rosalie drove up to see Bibbs was on a Sunday in late July. She wasn't sure if she'd tell him she'd broken up with him. She'd have to see how things went. In her wildest dreams, she and Bibbs would fight about him working, then Bibbs would get so mad he'd be willing to humiliate her. In reality, though, Rosalie felt depressed that it probably wouldn't happen that way. Bibbs didn't believe in any kind of strange sex. Sometimes Rosalie thought he didn't even like her pussy. She'd gotten a Brazilian wax for her last visit, and Bibbs had politely averted his eyes as one might for a birth defect.

Bibbs came out his front door just as Rosalie reached the end of his long, tree-shrouded drive. You could never sneak up on him because of his dog's acute hearing. Matthias always ran out and barked at Rosalie for a good minute until he remembered that he knew and liked her, then backed off and let Bibbs move in close.

Bibbs drove Rosalie wild, there was no denying it. She suspected she was somewhat unique in her response to him, though. Not that he was ugly or anything. He wasn't. He was handsome. Only Rosalie's standard of handsome, according to her friends, was somewhat skewed.

Bibbs dressed messily. He was tall, with weird, sprouting hair. Even though he was forty-three, all of his knuckles had rolls of skin like an old man's. Rosalie was fascinated by Bibbs's hands. They were much too strong. They could grip her very powerfully when they wanted, only Bibbs was usually stingy about this, except for when he was rubbing her back.

Today, he had shaved his beard down to a goatee, something Rosalie had requested. He was wearing her favorite jeans, an old pair of Levi's that sat beautifully on his ass, which, like his legs, was firm and tight.

"Shut the fuck up, Matthias!" he called from the porch, and eventually the dog fell silent. Bibbs came down the steps and put his arms around Rosalie. He had a hard-on, and she waited for him to lay her out on the hood of her car, raise her skirt (she had worn a skirt for this very reason), and fuck her standing up without concern for her orgasm. He didn't, though. He just sighed and said, "Oh baby. I've missed you."

They sat on the porch, and Bibbs opened a present Rosalie had brought him. It was an old, framed presidential ballot she had come across in an antique shop. The main choices were Herbert Hoover or Franklin D. Roosevelt. It was the kind of gift Rosalie resented having to give. When she saw it, naturally she couldn't turn it down. On the other hand, that gift was her nemesis. It represented everything about Bibbs that made her heart hurt.

"Wow," he said, gazing at the ballot. "This is really something."

"I'm glad you like it," Rosalie said. She was sitting on his lap in an old Adirondack chair.

"Please tell me you didn't pay a fortune."

"I can't tell you that," Rosalie said.

"Now I feel guilty," Bibbs said.

Rosalie thought there were plenty of other things for him to feel guilty about, but didn't say so.

Bibbs stared at the ballot a little longer, then set it aside. "How about dinner? I have a pizza in the oven."

"Can't we go upstairs?" Rosalie asked.

"The pizza will burn," Bibbs said, even though he'd reached a hand out and was rubbing her nipples through her shirt.

"Let's go upstairs," Rosalie said, leaning down and putting her mouth on his, and he said okay, that he'd turn off the oven.

In the bedroom, Rosalie told Bibbs straight out what she wanted. "I want you to tell me what to do," she said.

"What?" Bibbs said. He was lying on the bed naked, stroking himself, waiting to watch her undress.

"I want you to tell me what to do," Rosalie said again. "You be the boss and I'll do what you say."

"You don't know what to do?" Bibbs said, and he laughed a little.

"No," Rosalie said, "it's not that." She was quiet for a second, then said, "I want you to tell me what to do in a mean way."

Bibbs slowed down touching himself, then stopped altogether. "Wait," he said. "You mean, like, S and M?"

"I guess," she said. "Kind of."

"Huh," he said.

"What should I do, Bibbs?" Rosalie asked. She tried to sound sort of weak and pathetic.

"Well," he said. "I don't know."

"Should I touch myself?" Rosalie asked. This embarrassed her slightly, but she tried not to show it.

"I don't know," Bibbs said. He sat up on the edge of the bed. "I guess I'm not really sure this is turning me on."

"Oh," Rosalie said. She felt kind of humiliated, but not in the right way.

Bibbs reached for his shorts. "Let's have the pizza."

"Should I get down on my knees?" she asked.

"Rosalie," Bibbs said, pulling on his undershirt. "Could you please stop that?"

"Why?"

"I already told you," he said. "I'm just not into it."

"Then I want to break up," she said.

Bibbs looked at her. "You just got here. Don't be such an idiot. Jesus."

They went downstairs and had pizza. Rosalie sulked and would only eat the sausage off of her two pieces. "That's wasteful," Bibbs pointed out, and she told him sorry, but that she was on a high protein diet. It wasn't true, but she liked acting like there were things he didn't know about her, especially now that it felt like he knew too much.

The next morning, Bibbs went to work in the office behind his house. At lunch, he came in and said, "Want a sandwich?"

"No," Rosalie said. She was sitting in the living room, watching soap operas in her sweatpants. She added, "I'm probably going to head back home later today."

"What the hell are you talking about?" Bibbs said. He was holding a giant jar of mayonnaise. Bibbs always bought the largest size possible of everything, even though he was only one man.

"I just don't know what I'm supposed to be doing here," Rosalie said.

"What do you mean what you're supposed to be doing here? You're my girlfriend. You're here to visit. God."

"It doesn't feel like a visit."

"Rosalie," Bibbs said, "I'm not going to quit working, okay? This sabbatical was set up long before I met you."

"But I don't have anything to do," she said.

"Do your own work. You have plenty of work."

It was true, she did. She ran a graphic design business out of her apartment, and she owed one of her oldest clients, a travel magazine, a cover for their autumn issue. Every year it was pretty much the same: leaves, maple syrup, bed and breakfasts.

"I need my own office," Rosalie said, which was a lie. At home, she worked at her kitchen table. Only Bibbs would never have known that since he hadn't come to visit her yet.

"Well, go shopping then."

"For what?"

"I don't know. Whatever."

"Handcuffs?" Rosalie asked.

Bibbs hugged his jar of mayonnaise. "Listen," he said, "that stuff makes me really uncomfortable. I don't understand why you keep bringing it up."

"Can't you just tell me what to do?" she said. She muted the television and moved to the edge of the couch. She pushed her chest out a little.

"No," Bibbs said.

"Just one little thing?"

"Those are my choices? Either be a pervert or quit working?"

"You say what the choices are," Rosalie said.

"This is stupid," Bibbs said, turning to go back in the kitchen. "Fine. If you want to leave, fine."

After lunch, he went back out to his office, while Rosalie went upstairs and packed. She took her bags down to the car, then went to knock on Bibbs's door. He opened it, and Matthias, who always went to work with Bibbs, started barking.

"Shut up!" Bibbs yelled. "She's my fucking girlfriend!"

When it was quiet, Rosalie said, "I'm leaving."

Bibbs looked at her. He was furious, she could tell. He set his mouth so that his lips disappeared a little. Now would've been the perfect time for him to humiliate her, Rosalie thought, but instead he just said, "You are a very childish woman," and went back to his desk.

She went and stayed in a bed and breakfast in the town. The next day, she walked over to the rec center where Bibbs played his noon basketball game on Tuesdays and Thursdays. He saw her just as he sank a three-point shot from well behind the line. "Time out!" he called, and the other players looked at him like they didn't understand. When he started walking toward Rosalie, though, they dispersed and turned the other way.

Bibbs took Rosalie by the arm and ushered her out into a small hallway where there was a drinking fountain. "What the hell are you doing here?" he hissed.

"Watching you play basketball," she said. He was hurting her arm, and she had a fantasy that if she told him this, he would pinch her even harder. In reality, she knew that if she said anything he would simply let go.

"No," Bibbs said, "what are you doing in this town?"

"Nothing," she said.

"You said you were going home."

"I went to the bed and breakfast," she told him. "I was too tired to drive."

"Jesus Christ," he said. "This is lunacy."

She inhaled the smell of his sweat, which was too sweet and had taken some getting used to. Now, though, she craved it.

"Stop breathing like that," Bibbs said.

"Sorry."

"We'll talk about this at home," he said, then headed back into the gym.

"Wait," Rosalie said. "Are you telling me to go back to your place, or just asking?"

"This is all too much," he said. "You're taking this way too far."

"But I need to know."

He sighed. "Telling. Okay? You happy now? Get your ass back to my house."

He arrived home about forty-five minutes after she did. "Get out of the car," he barked, because that was where she was sitting. Once they were inside, she sat down on the couch, while he stood nearby, beside the gas stove. Finally he said, "Is it that you saw a movie about this stuff? Or you read a book?"

"No," Rosalie said.

"Then what is it?"

"Nothing," she said. "It was just an idea I had."

"Well, I don't want to do it," he said. "I think I've been pretty clear on that."

"Yes," she said, "you have."

"I think you know how I feel about you threatening to leave, too."

"I don't like it when you work," she told him.

"I have a grant!" he yelled.

Rosalie didn't say anything. She started to cry. She didn't know what was wrong with her, really. She didn't want Bibbs to work, but she didn't want to break up with him, either. The only thing that made it feel better in her head was if he would do mean things to her.

Bibbs sighed. Finally he said, "Okay. I won't work for the rest of the week. We'll do whatever you want, every day. We'll have adventures. How's that?"

Rosalie stopped crying and said okay.

The next day, Rosalie and Bibbs went to a mall and bought some new towels. Then they had lunch at a McDonald's drive-thru and drove home. "This is really boring," Bibbs said in the car. "I can't believe you would want your life to be this boring."

"I don't want it to be boring," Rosalie said.

"Well," Bibbs said, "too late."

They got off the highway and onto the rural roads that would lead to the dirt roads that would lead to Bibbs's place. It was pretty country, and Rosalie tried to imagine herself as one of its residents. She would have to drive a long way to get anywhere. If she and Bibbs fought in winter, it might only be possible to escape from him in snowshoes. If the pipes burst and there was flooding, she would have to act stoic about her stuff getting ruined.

On one of the rural roads, Bibbs noticed a large turtle trying to cross, and hit his brakes. He didn't even pull over—just stopped right there in the road. He hopped out of the car and Rosalie followed him. "I wish I had my camera," she said.

"You direct traffic," Bibbs told her, even though there was no one coming in either direction. He leaned down then and gripped the turtle's shell on either side, near the back feet. Rosalie thought this might make the turtle tuck its head in, but instead, it extended its neck fully and snapped its toothless jaw in the direction of Bibbs's left hand. All four of its feet were paddling the air, claws extended.

"You never take them back to the side of the road where they started," Bibbs announced, flinching a little against the turtle's writhing.

"Why not?" Rosalie asked.

"Because," he said, almost to the other side of the road. "They'll just try to cross again. Especially if it's a female. If it's a female, she might be laying eggs."

He vanished into the wild grass and hedges. When he reappeared a moment later, he was no longer holding the turtle, but blood gushed down his right arm. "Oh my God," Rosalie said.

"Get me one of those towels," Bibbs told her, gritting his teeth.

"Did she bite you?" Rosalie asked, opening the back door of the car and fishing around inside the Bed, Bath, & Beyond bag.

"No," Bibbs said. "Scratched."

Rosalie had to drive then. She took Bibbs to the hospital, where he required eight stitches in the very delicate spot between his index and middle fingers, then trailing down across his palm. The doctor told him that the scar would look like a new life line, but Bibbs didn't laugh. He said his hand really hurt. He said he had no fucking idea how he was going to type on his computer.

That night, Rosalie made dinner while Bibbs lay on the couch and watched TV. It was their usual rhythm, except without Bibbs feeling good after a day of work, and with his hand hurting. While the pasta boiled, Rosalie went to lie down with him, her backside pressed against his front. He wrapped his arms around her. It was like they were dying together.

Soon he moved his good hand over her breasts. He pulled her shirt up, then her bra, then he tugged at the fly of her jeans so that all the buttons popped open. He whispered, "You fucking cunt. You manipulative fucking cunt." He fucked her then, without regard for her orgasm, even though she came anyway. When he was done, he got up and went out to his office.

The next day he went to his office again, and Rosalie worked on her magazine cover at the kitchen table. They had lunch together at noon, and at six, she made dinner. Afterward, they went out on the porch to smoke a couple of cigarettes. Matthias joined them, laying his chin on Rosalie's bare feet. "He likes you," Bibbs said. "He may not recognize you all the time, but he likes you."

"Why doesn't he recognize me?" Rosalie asked.

Bibbs exhaled a stream of smoke. "It's an ocular problem."

Rosalie nodded.

"Put out your cigarette," Bibbs said a moment later.

She did.

He eased down in his chair and unbuckled his belt with his good hand. "Come over here."

Rosalie looked at him.

"Come over here," he said again. "My hand doesn't work. My dick is hard and my hand doesn't work."

Rosalie eased her feet out from under Matthias's chin and stood up.

"You make my dick hard," Bibbs said.

She walked across the porch toward him. He moved his legs apart, making a place for her, and she knelt down and took it. Soon, she felt his good hand in her hair, tangled up, gripping it. It didn't hurt, but she knew if she tried to take her mouth off of him, he wouldn't let her go.

The Sacrifice

Sarah Gorham

Memory is a ditzy court reporter:
You swear he was a good boy, the perfect
    little gentleman, though his cruelty,
    you admit, woke up
just as the day ended.
Now you shuffle your debts
    in order to appease him.
    You shake out your clothes
and pennies like a dozen
sad-faced clowns
    glower from the floor.
    Whatever can you do, when
so many bright collection agents
burn at the periphery?
    An invoice has been found.
    The sacrifice you pretend to love.

Would you like to see the house?

Sarah Gorham

murmured our chintz-clad hostess.
Oh yes and soon I was the faux client,
none of the cash required
to buy the house, were it for sale.
A grievous ache in my spleen
at the original blown-glass windows,
wide plank flooring and wainscotted
kitchen cabinets. Bathrooms for the hostess,
guests, children, gardener, even the dogs.
I wanted to pee. What would it take
to own such a house except some
personal tragedy, bad marriage, soul wasted
over stock options and lawyers fees?
But I liked our hostess and she had survived all that.
Onto the new addition with its water bed
the size of a lake, two overstuffed
chaise lounges just for thinking.
From the kitchen came the bouquet
of pepper and kalamata olive
encrusted lamb. My stomach whined
audibly, and I glanced around the room,
painted maroon just shy of bordello.
On the east wall was her "naked" collection,
voluptuous putti, Gauguin sketch, and photograph
of our host in a mud bikini. Yes,
you could see her breasts and I felt
a little hum begin in my toes, move teasingly

up my calves. Took a sudden step back
from our unembarasssed host.
Shall we? She gestured, sighing.
We followed her over the Persian carpet,
down the stairs buffed to a butterscotch glow.
But it was her gold and ruby cross
that directed my eye, distressingly,
straight into her cleavage. I didn't know
she was religious. So am I.

Dad
and my brother spent
all their time trying to figure out the
best way to utilize Mom's earnings. They usually did this
over continual rounds of tap stout at the Dew Drop Inn
downtown. Both had plenty of ideas but no initiative. Each night they'd come home exhausted
by the possibilities. (Strouse, page 193)

Seriidevüf

Nadine Nakanishi

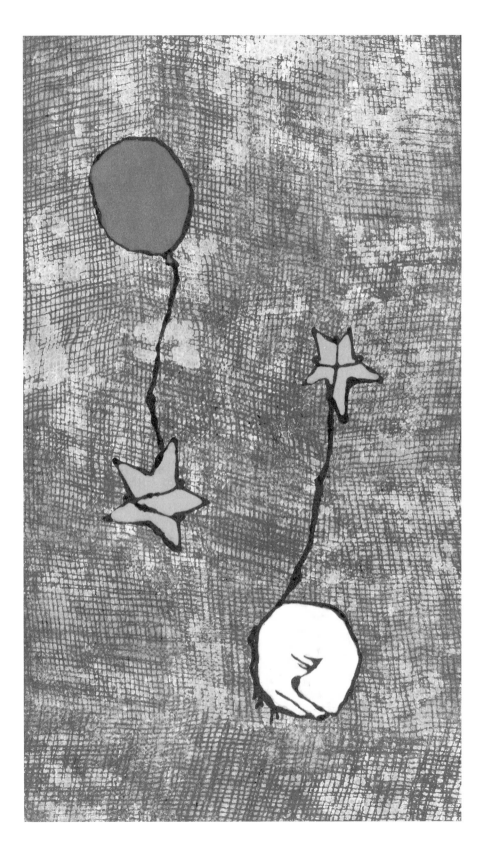

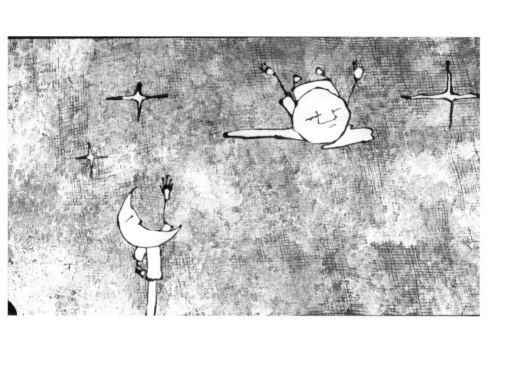

While Some Elegant Dancers Perched on Wires High Above a Dark, Dark Farm

Jennifer L. Knox

It must've been the poor Mexican kid
who left the radio on the porch, wrapped up
like a baby doll next to a fly-covered box
of pears gone all gooey. Some harvest—
but mother took it in as she took all things
in. Brother turned it on.

The first song was about love
on a bicycle ride and the notes warbled
like a bent rim under the rubber rolling along.
It was nice. The next song was about
a chocolate box from Paris full of love,
which was nice too, but as summer burned on then burned
its oily clunker of a motor out, the songs began sounding
all the same, only a little different, like the same

song was hiding underneath all the songs,
crooning the same stupid words out
its stupid gold caged speaker hole:
that *love* rhymed with *dove*
and more *boop bee doop* poop.
It never mentioned us once
or the winter coming on.

Mother tried cleaning it.
Brother tried punching it,
but at last Pop said, *Ask it
what it looks like on the outside,*
then wheeled himself from the room without looking
back to see if we got just
what he was getting at.
Did we ever.

Sophie in the Catacombs

Wendy Walker

I SPENT THE NEXT FEW DAYS IN THE TUNNELS, WORKING. THE wall to which I applied my efforts was quite recent, built of bones, six feet deep, laid perpendicular to the rock face, hiding it completely. Their ends made a knobby pattern reminiscent of crochet. I regarded the patches of order within the confusing whole and then allowed them to recede in the dim light.

Sometimes a belt of shadow would give me the clue to the hidden shape that held the mass together. My task—to construct a pattern that would dignify the bone wall—was a matter of clarifying what was already present. While I pondered I examined a heap of bones left behind by the workmen who had preceded me. I tried fitting similar bones together, first this way and then that. Interlocked pelvic bones formed rosettes that seemed to turn; jawless skulls stacked easily into columns. Little segments of spine made excellent garlands, but one piece alone could serve as a candlestick. I never tired of rotating bones with respect to each other, for this always produced surprising shapes. And rich as were the results of combining bones of the same type, juxtaposing different ones yielded even more curious possibilities. For instance, positioning skulls in the dense surface of knobs made those serried bulbs look like small heads struggling to emerge as the larger had; or I might take a few limbs from the pile and lay their length among the knobs. I'd find myself looking at boughs amidst heavy foliage then. The wall might have been a hedge, showered with ash or turned into salt.

I was never afraid in the tunnels. Many would have been discomfited by the presence of so many dead, but I found quiet and comfort there. Although occasionally I wondered whose jumbled skeletons I handled, I usually felt a milling crowd, unconscious of itself, intent on an object beyond my reach.

But a few days later, I was suddenly overcome by dread. I tried to continue fitting a limb into place, but the wall seemed to lurch; I stared at the bones and understood, through my fingers, their innocence. Yet destruction leaned over me and my materials, and I was no more significant than they. Disaster was setting us at an equal distance, me and the bones, not aside, but readied. Have I described it? I sensed determination, coming through but not from the bones. They and I together were being viewed as opponents, and a game was in progress, although we didn't know it.

The following afternoon, when the mood in the tunnels had settled back into its course, I had to ask myself what had happened to disturb that calm.

Fear had intruded itself, but of what, I couldn't say. I kept at the question, worrying it fruitlessly, and left my work a perfect shambles. A day later, as I sorted bones and tried to recapture the logic of my design, I shrank from those circling thoughts. Then I tried talking to myself as a mother would: a young woman should spend less time with the dead, and more with the living, the younger, the better. Hearing that firm voice I wondered whether my mind had not finally rebelled against too many workmen's jokes about cheap building materials.

Night Thoughts (I)

Trevor Dannatt

Waking at three, still hearing
Last night's music, joyful singing
I wish for tea and slipper shod
Find stairs and moonlight cold
Casting black shadows where I tread.
The disc floats free, entrancing, high
But to the East vapor trails sully
           the planished sky

Night Thoughts (II)

Trevor Dannatt

Thin wraiths of cloud, flecked and lucent,
Far vacant space with single star.
How many mindless years were spent
To reach here, surely some place there?
Unlikely, but it shimmers yet,
Gives wonder, heralds faith and doubt.

Braised Beef for Three

Giuseppe O. Longo

Translated from the Italian by David Mendel

BUT SHE WAS ONE JUMP AHEAD OF ME, WITH THAT TELEPHONE call she had anticipated all the moves I had thought of making for years, or better, the moves that I might have made in some vague far distant future, for example to propose that we get together again (deep down it was the only move I had in mind) and I had imagined that affected by this proposition she would have cried out and would have accepted me saying that she had been expecting this moment for years, and even I, touched, would have squeezed out a few tears and would have embraced her awkwardly and with emotion, saying now, now don't cry, you'll see that everything will come out all right, we have made a long detour, a diversion of thirty or forty years to find ourselves together again and things like that, instead that Monday morning she phoned me and gave me this news, which was both a request and an announcement, almost a wedding invitation, and there she left me to think about it, to reflect how and in what way in all those years, and particularly in the last years, I had made illusions for myself about her, and about myself too, in fact about both of us I had built up these ideas which (at a stroke) had shown themselves to be not only mistaken but also puerile if not actually idiotic.

And so she wants a divorce, Guido does not just ask but rather states, putting down his Coca-Cola can. He says, women are, as usual, better, stronger, and more practical than men, and I must admit he is right, for years I had toyed with the idea of asking for a divorce myself, but I never did it, I never asked her, to avoid what she called in a rather melodramatic but effective way the ultimate outrage (I agree I didn't ask her also and perhaps above all to leave open a way out, the possibility of returning etc., etc.), and instead it happens that I return from Paris one night and the morning after I receive this call in which she asks me for a divorce and tells me of her intention to remarry, and I naturally lacked the courage to oppose it, without even thinking about it I said that I would certainly agree to it, divorce, just imagine, after so many years of separation, in spite of all the phone calls and the many dinners in restaurants to tell each other our troubles with a strange if not suspect or even sick complicity, after so much dissipation and, at times, even desperation, I said to her, on the spur of the moment, certainly I'll give you a divorce, and at the time, in spite of the surprise, it seemed to me to be quite the most reasonable thing in our situation, and when I told Guido about it (saying, just look at the mistaken ideas I had about my wife, I thought she would wait there for me and instead . . .), he approved my conduct, my conduct had been very reasonable, he said, in our situation the most reasonable thing was in fact divorce, so that at least one of us (that's to say her) could remake a life for herself (he actually said it like that, just as you read in women's magazines) and then perhaps the other (that's to say me) would find the force or the courage or the freedom of spirit to remake a life for himself.

But I had no intention of remaking a life for myself, I had tried too many times to remake my life, I had tried to remake my life with various women but it had never worked out, so, notwithstanding the fact that I was by now over fifty, after that phone call I felt an irresistible impulse to abandon myself to mindless pleasure (I had said amuse myself, but Guido had actually used that expression, which according to him corresponded better to the facts and to the image he had built up of me over the years, Guido regards me as an old lunatic, and saying mindless pleasure he had looked me up and down suspiciously with an air of both complicity and reproof), in short that phone call had brought on the fantasy of mindless pleasure and so I at once set about looking up my old girlfriends, I took steps to make some new ones, to get to know other women, especially young ones, secretaries and clerks and lady doctors from the Hospital Service and aspiring writers, I wasn't very selective, and I invited them to dinner, some agreed to spend the evening at my place, without however giving me much. I felt their curiosity but also a certain diffidence, I debated between this woman and that without making up my mind, and this dispersion of energy certainly did not advance what seemed to me to be my purpose (but what does this old man want from me, these women must have asked themselves, Guido observed, opening himself another can of Coca-Cola, he drinks only Coca-Cola and, when he's ill, only fully aerated mineral water), but what my aim really was, I myself perhaps did not know.

And then, from where had this music teacher now sprung, this species of long-haired failed artist, with dandruff and a bent and narrow back (but no, it was I who saw him in this way, it was I who imagined he might be a music teacher, a musician, one of Chagall's fiddlers who take off into the sky legs up with their violet or red instrument in their hand, and on the head the beret of a Jewish railwayman and below there is a wooden cabin and a meadow where a blueish cow grazes), in reality I had never seen him, my wife's future husband, and even referring to him as such annoyed me a lot and I didn't even know what his job was, whether he was an elementary-school teacher or a mailman, and the fact that she had defined him as patient and discreet incited me if not to animosity, at least to sarcasm and in reaction I had started going out with all those women, in a demented paroxysm of erotic origin (Guido) in which the only loser was me. I barely managed between appointments, I made each of them think she was the only one, I talked a lot and above all I listened, pretending an interest in their ups and downs at work, in their problems with their feet or their thyroids, in their family arguments, I listened to their worries and to their aspirations in life, it seems incredible, but each one had some trouble with the office supervisor or with her mother or with her weight, and there I was listening while I was dying to sleep and thinking that the next day I had to go to Naples or Milan for a conference or to make a presentation while this woman persisted in telling me that she only wanted a less thankless job, a little independence from her mother etc., etc.

I would like you to meet him, my wife said one day on the phone, I had always been too agreeable with her, and this time too I said yes, perhaps in order to be forgiven for some of my many wrongs, it's well known that expiation is a great comfort, but when you think about it she too had done me wrong quite a number of times (as I had often explained to Guido), for example many years earlier, when we were still together, there was that affair with the Sicilian doctor, a matter which had made me suffer a good deal, but since she too had suffered a good deal, I didn't know whether to credit that episode to my account or to mark it down as a draw, the fact is that I said yes, that I accepted her invitation to dinner with the fiancé, and while feeling all the debasement of my docility, there was nevertheless in me a vague well-being, similar to the titillation with which certain lower beings greet the satisfaction of their basic needs (marvelous to feel yourself a worm), and I told myself too that for one evening I would spare myself the verbal skirmishes with my friends, I would avoid for once dispensing my pearls of wisdom, there's no need to search outside yourself, rather look within, the truth is always a dangerous achievement, read Marcus Aurelius again, for God's sake, exclaimed Guido, but I had no need of his sarcasm to realize that all this was a clear manifestation of stupidity.

And so she organized a dinner at her house, my wife had always been a good hostess and a perfect cook, and she said to me that her house seemed to her to be the only neutral territory for such a tricky meeting, or better the only common ground that I and this fiancé and future husband could have, and I will make braised beef she said, so I had even decided to buy her flowers, a bunch of roses (yellow, I decided, having consulted a book on the language of flowers and having spoken about it to Guido), and it seemed to me that arriving with flowers for the woman who for so many years had been my companion (in bed too, naturally) I would have given a signal of friendship and peace, but before arriving at the house I had abandoned the roses on the steps of a supermarket, I had looked for a church, at first a church had seemed to me to be more suitable for abandoning the flowers, but in this zone churches were scarce and then a supermarket gave the whole thing a more aseptic air, when you think about it a church smelt too much of matrimony and sanctity, but we had broken matrimony and sanctity and we continued to break them, at least according to the teachings of the church, thus the supermarket was better.

Having parked the car in a small square, I slowly covered the hundred meters that separated me from my wife's house, and meanwhile all the women I had been with in that period came to mind, whose number had unexpectedly increased after the famous Monday morning phone call in which my wife had announced her intention to remarry and I had given her what one might call my blessing, while the women I went with for one reason or another hadn't given me their blessing. Gianna didn't give it to me because in this period sex didn't interest her, as I told Guido, Marina didn't give it to me because we still don't know each other well enough, Michela because we knew each other too well, Esther because she was afraid of getting involved, Patricia because she gives it only when she is very involved, Guido drank Coca-Cola and listened, he drank long gulps straight from the can, every now and again he nodded his approval, but after a while, after I had given him enough insignificant details, and the details of this story seemed for the most part insignificant (for example I told him that with all this talking I was doing I had begun to confuse these women's problems and thus I said or asked of Marina what I should have asked or answered Esther or Daniela, with results which you can imagine), and confronted with these insignificant details Guido started to sneer and to mutter mild insults, like chronic infantilism, incipient idiocy, fornicator's cretinism, senile impotence.

So, thinking about all these stupid things, I had found myself in front of the supermarket, which is actually under my wife's flat and it seemed more honest to me, and perhaps more gentlemanly and postmodern, to leave there the expensive bunch of yellow roses that I had bought for her, more so because Guido had said that on no account should I take the flowers myself, flowers you send, and these words had created a certain unease inside me, tempered only by the knowledge that I could rid myself of the flowers at any time, while if I had sent them, there would have been nothing further I could do, it had been in fact one of my tested tactics to keep an escape route open (Guido), and while I rang the bell and entered the hallway and waited for the lift and then went up to the fifth floor, I imagined my wife already divorced and remarried, I imagined her flourishing and at peace, in position at last to pontificate as she likes to do, without contradiction, to pour out her wisdom and her goodwill, because that lout of a husband she had found for herself was certainly accommodating and tactful, he was certainly dominated by my wife, or by his wife, or by both, since she was the same person.

This husband seemed to me to be a perfect idiot from the beginning, and his holding my wife's hand in an adolescent manner seemed to me pathetic and too allusive of an intimacy that aimed to exclude me, notwithstanding the invitation that I had simple-mindedly accepted. His obvious stupidity nevertheless did not attenuate my gratitude to him, a gratitude that I had unexpectedly felt a day or two earlier during one of my usual colloquia with Guido and that did not derive so much from the imminent liberation this man was offering me from a difficult and complaining woman (a ball and chain as Guido had defined her with his usual frank precision), from a woman who knew very well how to use the weapon of moral blackmail, my gratitude to this man derived, above all, from the fact that very shortly he would put an end to that monthly bloodletting of the check I had to send my wife by order of the Court of Trieste, to which I had always scrupulously conformed, in fact, very shortly he would have to maintain her, my wife, that is his wife, he would acquire a fine scrawny hen to pluck, this man with the spectacles and the swollen face of an old cirrhotic seated in front of me, posing, pouring out wine for me and cutting bread for me, as if that wine and that bread had not been bought by my wife with the money I had given her only two weeks before, but the idea that in a few weeks or months that man would have on his hands a scrawny hen to pluck brought on in me an irrepressible joy, now the scrawny hen is yours, I told him scornfully, and my wife, that is to say my ex-wife, that is his fiancée, or his future spouse, in fact all these women transfixed me with a look to kill, a look I knew so well, but he, the fiancé, boor that he was, lacked the courage to give me the reply I deserved, so he smiled stupidly with his fork in midair, but that was his problem, not only his inability to give me a reply, but also the scrawny hen that he would soon have to pluck, these were his problems and I didn't worry too much about them, except that for some reason that still escapes me, the unpleasant sensation grew upon me that I was the imbecile, I had for a moment the feeling that in some way I was selling off my wife on monthly terms, those terms in fact that in a couple of months from now I would no longer have to pay, the loser, definitely, in this whole business, perhaps was no one but myself.

Amid all these thoughts the conversation proceeded with difficulty and I think my wife was expecting something more lively of the first encounter between her two husbands, a first encounter that for me could be the last, considering the spirit I found in that man who really did look like a Chagall fiddler even though he was a doctor (meanwhile I had learned from my wife that he was a highly respected gastroenterologist), my wife, you see, has a passion for doctors, she specializes in doctors (Guido), and perhaps that is not a coincidence, given that our conjugal life had the stamp of disease, our married life and then our separated life too was played out under the banner of disease and pathology, not only physical pathology, because my wife has always somatized the suffering that I inflicted upon her, which living with me or separation from me brought on, in fact everything about me made her suffer, among our friends she was famous for her spastic colon, a psychosomatic spasticity resistant to any cure either conventional or homeopathic, but the signs of pathology were not limited to the colitis, in her to the colitis, in me to psoriasis (after we got married I always suffered from psoriasis), no, there were, too, hidden but no less revealing signs, signs that were, so to speak moral, or spiritual, of pathology, as Guido once said our life had been a long, interminable experiment in pain of the soul and disease of the soul, of which we two were both the observers and the guinea pigs.

Meanwhile the braised beef had appeared on the table. I had always been very flattering about my wife's braised beef, but the wine I had drunk so copiously from the first course onward, the uneasiness that the shiny and flabby cheeks of the betrothed medico provoked in me and the increasingly nervous demeanor of my wife, prevented me from savoring in the usual way this dish in which were combined the culinary skills of whole generations of housewives (my wife's housewife antecedents, on both the mother's and the father's sides had belonged to the most diverse and disparate races; they had spoken all languages and eaten all European foods and from these ethno-linguistic and culinary crosses this dish had miraculously arisen), a dish that was handed down from mother to daughter, and was a notable part of the dowry that the family passed on to young brides, but notwithstanding this illustrious lineage, that evening the braised beef seemed to me to be tough and stringy, insipid and at the same time over-seasoned, but certainly it was I who wasn't functioning, my palate had rebelled at my brain's travail and demanded more attention, but how could I devote my attention to the braised beef if my mind was filled with the ugliest memories of my life, for example my father came to mind, when they found the tumor in his lungs, and when I was alone I cried, but when I was with him I feigned levity, but he knew, he certainly knew, because he responded in monosyllables, he no longer laughed at my jokes, no longer revealed those yellow crumbling teeth, roasted by the hundred thousand cigarettes he had smoked in a lifetime and I realized that he would soon leave me an orphan and no one would any longer defend me or advise me on life's dangers, for example no one had advised me on how to treat my wife to prevent that small amount of marriage that remained to us after breaking up, not that I had ever asked advice from my father, but all told he was there, and behind his presbyopic's thick glasses swam two amazed and generous eyes, which soon I would no longer be able to see.

Meanwhile I ate the braised beef and continued drinking, my wife's medico and betrothed continued to pour wine for me with an alarmed though satisfied air. I don't know why he was so satisfied, if anyone should have been satisfied it should have been me, who at a stroke would be freed from my ball and chain and from the necessity to pay the monthly check, and in fact, since they had already made the decision and I hadn't opposed it, indeed conceding to my wife divorce and freedom, it came to me that I should be able to suspend payment of the check at once, that is to say Chagall's old fiddler could start at once to pluck his scrawny hen, you could begin at once to pluck your hen, I said to him, raising my glass and proposing a toast, but he didn't respond, he stiffened somewhat and my wife got up and placed herself behind the chair of her betrothed medico, as if to protect him or to make a bloc against me, in effect to signify to me that she was his ally and that the business with me was really finished and once again I imagined my wife's future, an unperturbed and peaceable life, standing shoulder to shoulder with her tranquil gastroenterologist (like in those wedding photos of yesteryear, shot against a richly folded curtain, in the foreground a tiny table on which the wife rests a languid hand, whilst the husband stares at the lens with the grim satisfaction of a husband), who perhaps would at last find a remedy for her spastic colon, while I would continue my life of dissipation with secretaries and employees with low erotic yield, scratching my psoriasis and perhaps even contracting in my turn a legend-worthy spastic colon.

The braised beef neither came up nor went down despite my having helped it down with the generous doses of wine that the betrothed groom was pouring for me, the atmosphere was getting more relaxed. My wife had sat down but I was becoming sad again, I thought not only of my father, but also of my mother who had died a couple of years ago in a squalid hospice, and I also thought about my grandmother, who had passed away many years before on a day when the bora was blowing. It didn't seem possible to die on such a day, with all that sunshine, in that whirlwind of autumn leaves, from the window of her large room in the Maddalena Hospital I saw a sliver of blue sea and I repeated to myself, it's the sea grandma, it's the sea and I myself didn't even know what it was I wanted to say, but obviously her death tormented me and I had to do something to pull myself up, so much so that a few weeks later my wife surprised me when I was making love to my secretary and she was devastated, the more so because my secretary was paralyzed and got about in a wheelchair and in order to make love to her I had placed her on the desk and was maneuvering her as best I could, only my wife hadn't grasped the comic side of the affair and was mortally offended, really thinking about it perhaps there were no comic aspects, she kept repeating it's disgusting, it's disgusting, and then with that poor girl, even if really that poor girl got along pretty well, given her condition, in short our war began at that moment, but it wasn't a real war, because deep down we loved each other and we tried to help each other, that is each helped the other to harm himself and the other, but with infinite tenderness, a heedless and sweet euthanasia.

When the incident with the secretary came into my mind I started to laugh, and this hearty laughter almost made me choke on the braised beef so much so that my wife this time got up and stood behind me and started to slap me lightly on the back, but it didn't do any good, I continued to cough but it pleased me that she was worried about me, and even the medico after a while came to slap my back and I felt I was the center of attention, the cough was destroying me but I felt really good, I felt that diffuse well-being of a stroked cat (a large handsome tabby cat, spread out on an armchair close to the stove, on a winter afternoon, the day is ending but no one has yet switched on the light), I would have liked to have purred and said incoherent things, but the braised beef was still there choking me, and I must have had a strange look because at a certain point the medico pulled my head back, stuck two fingers down my throat and pulled out a short but wide and twisted tangle of pale stringy meat, half-chewed, the mouthful I had tried in vain to swallow with the aid of wine, and he put it on my plate, in the middle of the braised beef, which I hadn't yet finished. I knew that today the braised beef hadn't come out well, I was thinking, it hadn't been any good at all today, the braised beef I mean, and I began to have vague stomach pains, but I certainly didn't want to vomit, to vomit in my wife's house, before her future husband, would have been an obvious and vulgar outrage, even if deep down, deep down it would not have displeased me to make clear my disgust with this little family scene in which I had been invited to take part.

Anyhow I did not vomit and I forced myself to talk of other things, I started by saying that I was writing a story, imagine a Savoia-Marchetti seaplane set down in a large square, under a 1930s sun, around it are long low buildings, in the Fascist style, a sort of Cinecittà reconstruction, near the airplane some Japanese aviators are standing, with little flags and handkerchiefs tied to their collars and to their epaulets, which are whipping in the wind, stretched like small bird's wings, the aviators have leather helmets, the chin strap is not fastened and it too is flapping, imagine that sunshine, that blue sky, then something must happen, but I don't yet know what it is, the medico stared at me without understanding, a bit concerned, my wife stared at some point on the table, her lovely blue eyes dull and absent, but I did not give up and because I felt reassured, I push to one side the chewed up piece of whitish meat that had almost choked me, and I started again to eat the braised beef saying it isn't that bad, this braised beef, it's not one of your best but it isn't too bad, really, perhaps my wife didn't even hear me, but the fiancé looked at me gratefully for that offer of an armistice, as he interpreted it, and gave me an inane smile, perhaps at that point I could also have told him about the boy with the protruding eye who looked at himself all the time in the mirror, training himself to make it stick further and further from its orbit, to make it a real telescope or periscope, that's it, a periscope to spy on the gymnastics mistress when she goes to the toilet and sits with her fine and fleshy white buttocks, and this eye slides up the wall and enters by the small window and aims at the seated woman who urinates gently and then stands up again and bends, exhibiting once again her large moon shaped buttocks etc., etc., but I didn't know whether a story like that would interest the gastroenterologist, it would however have pleased my wife, then, when we were together we would tell it to each other in bed, while making love, always inventing new details, erotic fantasies, how much I wanted to turn back and start from the beginning, with my wife or with someone else, it's not important, but start from the beginning (which is actually a form of senile impotence, Guido would say, and in fact when I tell him these things he says that it is a form of senile impotence).

It is true that I felt a sort of nostalgia for my wife, but it was a strange nostalgia, without object, it was like regret for something that never was, something that I had created for myself, a figment of the imagination, and certainly she too had felt that empty regret for all those years, which however had served remarkably well to keep us suffering, and we passed this suffering from one to the other, when one of us suffered he or she sought out the other and found relief, regaining a minimum of tranquillity, almost of happiness, making the other suffer and went away leaving the other in the pit of pain, and while the medico was telling my wife to reheat the mountain of braised beef which remained and my wife, like a good wife obediently returned to the kitchen with the enormous oval dish loaded with meat and gravy, I searched my memory for some husband figure to inspire my demeanor, it was not easy for me to adopt a line of conduct that was at the same time detached and participatory as it seemed to me the circumstances required, and so I rummaged in my memories or in the memories of my reading to see if there was some husband who in analogous circumstances had behaved himself in a correct and dignified way, I was looking for a model of a husband or a model husband, but finding nothing it occurred to me that a little earlier the gastroenterologist had laid hands on me, if only with good intent, in order to prevent me choking on the braised beef, and that he was a doctor and so in a certain sense authorized to lay hands on the first comer, if only with good intent, this license of his to touch and to grope in a way that was actually invasive, to enter into the body and the throat of others, and even into other people's bellies, this sort of social authorization I did not feel myself in the least willing to grant him, I thought resentfully, if it had been up to me I would not have conceded to anyone the authority to poke his nose into other people's business, especially in mine, everyone should stay on his own side of the street without looking to either side, without interfering, to say nothing of the much trumpeted solidarity in the name of which everyone maintains that he should and could poke his nose into other people's business, all the more so in this case, since if he had not intervened with his medical skill and I had choked there, in front of the two mature fiancés, what sort of a lesson would it have been for them, choking to death I would have been able to savor not only the too insipid and at the same time too strong taste of that unsuccessful braised beef, but also the extremely sweet honey of the vendetta, but what honey, what vendetta, Guido exclaims when I tell him everything, vendetta for what and against what, if not against yourself, choking to death you would spite only yourself, he says pouring himself a Coca-Cola, this time in a white plastic cup, and in addition, he says, you have never been able to hold on to a woman, you have never been able to hold on to a woman for more than a couple of months, at most a year, you have thrown away everything that life has given to you.

Meanwhile my wife had returned carrying the oval dish of braised beef with her arms raised and outstretched in a priestly and almost triumphal gesture, her eyes sparkling, she hoped that after all the evening would right itself and tried to contribute with an air of forced cheerfulness, but I did not join in the deception, I was quite decided not to make myself an accomplice in this conspiracy between her and her betrothed, and while the steaming braised beef was placed at the center of the table, in the midst of the ordered disorder, my eye suddenly fell upon the little jar of strong paprika and I began to sprinkle strong paprika on the new portion of braised beef that my wife had given me with the aid of the medical violinist, I swallowed a mouthful, I prepared myself another one and I continued to strew the meat and the gravy with strong paprika, I felt the mucous membrane of my mouth catch fire, under my skin I felt the formication of sweat, I felt my eyes almost escaping from their orbits like the periscopic eye of the young eavesdropper, from the roots of my hair to the tips of my fingers came boilings and flushings, but I continued to swallow paprika and braised beef with a threatening voracity, I threatened those two with my voracity and with the little jar of strong paprika that I brandished and continued to scatter on the brown shiny dripping chunks of braised beef, that never ending braised beef, my wife must have made pounds and pounds, perhaps she had got a bargain, an unforeseen discount, the butcher had decided to sell off the beef and she had taken advantage of it, the fact was that all this brown beef, veined with fat, rich in violet-gold reflections under the low chandelier, that mountain whose color and steamy humidity reminded me of hot and secret bodily parts, that tremulous mass of meat aroused in me a mixture of repugnance and greed, because of which I continued to eat of it with a growing sense of nausea that was ready to overcome me, and I thought to myself, the butcher's emporium, the chopping block, the bed, arousing in me bestial images of abattoirs, of fresh blood, of sheep, slaughtered Minotaurs, and I started to murmur flesh, sacrificial victim, flayed alive, mutilation, Calvary, and I felt sad with a cosmic sadness, irremediable, the waves of paprika set my hair on fire, I was overtaken by an uncontrollable trembling of the hands, my eyes wept, I sweated blood, I was on the cross, my hands transfixed by huge rusty nails, on my head the crown of thorns, until everything went black and I fainted, they told me later, my face in the plate of tepid braised beef, my forehead, hair and nose in the gravy, brown, thick, and fat.

Guido sighs, he offers me a glass full of Coca-Cola, he drinks from the can, sighs and shakes his head, what should I have done, I ask him, and he sighs, perhaps I should have competed for my wife with the violinist, I should have confronted him, bared my chest and fought with him, torso against torso, imagine it, two middle-aged men you might even say old, flaccid, who struggle over an old woman, a pathetic scene, imagine it, to feel his hands on me once again, his skin, smelling his rancid odor, of sweat, the smell of the medicines he handles, imagine it, I have never fought in my life, not even when I was little, I tried to resolve quarrels with reason, I took it from everyone, should I start now, and for what, to reconquer a woman who deep down means nothing to me, if she had been important everything would have been different from the beginning. Guido stares fixedly at me, shakes his head and takes another sip from the can, looks at me again then says, all told it seems to me that braised beef wasn't that good, then he bursts out laughing, and meanwhile a sweet breeze blows up from the Russian steppes and from the blue cabins and lifts up Chagall's fiddler and carries him away with his scrawny hen to pluck, with his beret, with the red violin, in an ineffable levitation, through scattered puffy clouds and little rainbows.

The Green Bench

Matvei Yankelevich

    The green bench
the silence of
afternoon
the green grass
all of us are cars
or, all of us are ears

then, when all
is said and then
all is gone, another
afternoon, like
all others   back to the
scroll, back to the
asphalt season

    The green bench
sits in the
green grass
and everyone is eyes
every one blade
dilated, cast
for the role of
shadow, left behind
I like this to be strange

to leave off
left behind on the green
green grass sits
the green bench
again and again
afternoon

       Why come back? Keep
silent? Does anybody want
a bench except to sit on? This
green grass, except perhaps to run
a finger through soft blades?

       There's nothing at all
special here. Neither particular, nor
particularly vague. Bah, lyric! It's
just that I, too, am a little lovesick.
It's not your fault, green bench.

  It is not the fault of grass
nor the fault of afternoon
still morning, already
late night, and outside is no
green, but verging   don't
let the afternoon fool you
it comes back to
bore you

who are
cold and seek boredom's
green bending
who are
weak and can't quite quit
an ending

Male Order

Norman Douglas

THE BLAST IS MADE OUT OF THE SAME BRICK AS THE HIGH
school, but it's only two stories with no windows and the walls are
painted gray under the graffiti we scrawl along Pine Street and back
in the alley where the bands and the beer come in. The Blast is the
only place we can go to hear hardcore and hang out without morons
and punk bashers screwing around. Course, there's always a few skinheads, but you can handle them once they get used to you some. You
can get into the Blast if you have no ID, but the bartenders are real
strict about serving and none of the older kids want to see the place
busted over some squirt trying to get tight. A lot of people even say
the cops are paid to stay away, which is fine with us. All that makes no
difference, since we always find someone to buy for us before we get
there. So, we either get cocked on the way or sneak in pints and halves
and slug away crouched close to the floor in some corner or the middle of the wheel. The wheel is where you crash and burn. Kids are
skanking or doing the worm or just rocking. Sometimes you get
beaned by a dive or someone gets too drunk or stoned and it's a mess
of puke all over and the floor is not big. I love the wheel. All the black
and rags flap by, palefaces and fists and terror in the eyes, sometimes
spots of blood might be yours but you know there is no telling till the
next day.

Rich is five years older than me. I met him a couple years back
when I first started hanging out at the Blast and drinking. Noel was
my best friend back then instead of Sully, who is my best friend now.

Rich would buy for me and Noel back then no problem, a lot of the time turning us on to pot. People say Rich was a great basketball player as a freshman. He never said much about it. We never asked. They say the coach asked Rich to be captain of the junior-varsity team his sophomore year. He never showed for tryouts. Not that I blame him. For all I care, you can take all the stupid sports in the world and drive them a long way off a short pier. I guess this was a big drag for Rich, though—everyone started to call him a faggot just because he refused to jump around the gym trying to put this stupid ball in some hole twice his height from the floor. People will call you a fag for all kinds of senseless reasons. People call me a fag sometimes just because I dress a little different. Not people really, but rednecks and jocks and assholes like that; the black kids will laugh because to them, punk means fag. I just ignore the whole army of idiots, unless they get in the way.

The thing that was sort of embarrassing was that Rich did more than just buy for me and Noel. I can never remember how it got started—I must have blocked it out of my memory—but when there was nothing else to do and we were hanging around Rich's place, sometimes we would give each other head. That was a couple years ago, and not something I really like to talk about. I feel like I should, though, since people say that anyone could be queer and that you should never feel like anything is wrong with it if you are, or if your friends are. My mom swears I have homophobia, but she has no idea what went on back then. Well, maybe she does, but even if she did know, and maybe since it did happen, I would never say I was homophobic. On the other hand, even though it did happen, I would never say I was a homosexual either. But only because I'm not.

The weird part about what me and Noel and Rich did was that I never looked at it as being queer or homosex or anything. I mean, I never talked about it or looked forward to it or anything. We just did it. We talked about the kinds of girls we thought were good looking and how we wanted to screw them and Rich would tell us about girls he met or went out with or balled or whatever. But at some point, he would always start it off by asking us if we wanted to do it, just like that, "You guys wanna do it now?" And we would just say, yeah. Then we would do it in some kind of order with two of us going at it while the other guy read a comic book by himself or maybe even watch kind of detached like, and then we switched after the first guy would nut and go like that till it was over with all three of us kind of satisfied, so to speak. It was all pretty normal, like masturbation, except there was somebody else with you. Like the way you toss off, you just come and forget about it. That was how it was with these guys. When we finished, we would go on talking or drinking or smoking pot and listening to Rich's stereo like nothing ever happened.

One day when Rich gave me a ride home, my mom was coming up the sidewalk in front of our house. She looked at us and got this look on her face like she wanted to talk but forgot how, like if you have a nightmare and try to scream but don't, and when you wake up it turns out to be too late. I got out of the car, an old convertible Corsair with the top down on account of it being one of those beautiful spring days that gets everyone so delirious and happy-go-lucky. Rich drove off without being introduced and when I said Hi to her, my mom right off asked me who he was. I told her it was Rich and then for some reason I got all embarrassed about everything with Rich and Noel. To change the subject, I asked where she was coming from, which was obviously the market, as she had two brown paper shopping bags in the little rolling handcart. She tried to act normal, but I could tell she was as uncomfortable as I was. When she got the door open, I took the cart from her, and on the way upstairs, she asked me the regular questions about school and what I did after, to which I gave the normal answers, like saying school was stupid and after school I did nothing. She told me to put the groceries away and went to her room to yak on the phone, for which I was grateful. As soon as I had the groceries put away, I split to my room and pretended to read until dinner. What I really did then was decide that this threesome of me and Rich and Noel was for sure too weird to keep going. Mom never mentioned Rich again, but it was a little uptight between us at dinner that night. In the morning, though, things were back to normal.

The next time I saw Rich was about a week later, and he never asked if I wanted to mess around or anything. It was like he knew I would say no. The whole time he just bitched about money. He was selling too little pot to make his unemployment worthwhile. He was bummed out that he might have to work. Rich had his bass in his lap like he was about to play it, but he never did. When he ran out of things to say, he would pluck at the strings nervously, but not playing really. We smoked reefer, and when I split he gave me a joint he said was laced with heroin. I took it over to Noel's and we puffed it up and made like elephants on a goofball kick all afternoon. I never told Noel how I had enough of the messing around, but he seemed to figure it out, too.

It was around that time I started to go out with Collette Smith. I hung around her because she loved to make out, and, to be honest, I had never done it before, so I decided she would be a good way to learn. She already had a reputation, but when I told Rich about it, he said to forget about the kids at school. He said not everybody gets a reputation, and everybody gets laid sooner or later, one way or another, like it or not. He said I would be lucky and I should be thankful if Collette let me do it with her. He bet that would give me a head start on almost everybody in my class. Besides, he said, if she let me do it, she must like me, since girls hardly ever do it with guys they hate. Collette and me broke up after only a couple months, though. I guess I should say she broke up with me one day when I called her a slut for no good reason. I told her I was only joking and I hardly meant it but she knew all about that reputation and what the other kids said about her. She told me she was nothing to joke about.

By the end of that little affair, I almost never saw Rich and I was so sick of the secret that I totally avoided Noel, even in the cafeteria. Rich might see me with some friends at the Blast or in the park and ask if we needed drugs or anything but I would say no right off, even if we were looking. This happened lots of times, until one time I was with Sully and Garth. They got riled up at me, asking what the hell was my problem. I told them Rich was a fag, that once he asked me for a blow job. They laughed and asked me if I did it. I lied and said I never sucked anybody's pecker and that nobody never sucked mine. Garth wanted to know what about Collette. I ignored him and Sully asked what my beef was with Rich if there was no dick-licking going on between us; if a guy says he can get booze or dope, it makes no difference if he does the bufu or not. Anyways, he said, if he ever asked us to do it, we could kick his ass or get somebody else to do it, turn him over to some rednecks or jocks.

So, Rich started to buy for us again. I mostly hung with him and Sully. Noel never came around and we never talked about him and there was no funny stuff. Rich really was okay and had dynamite drugs he gave us mostly for free. He was no sissy, either, and he went out with this beautiful super skinny girl from Pawtucket named Mary. She only has two years on me, and when she was going with Rich, she would scratch my head all affectionate and monkey-like and kiss me a sweet goodbye right smack on my mouth when she left with him. I sure liked her.

Sully made jokes about Rich and Mary, but only if we were someplace without them, and I laughed with him a lot, sometimes making jokes myself. We even called Rich "The Fag" behind his back, but it was really mostly sour grapes that he had the experience and Mary the beautiful girl and all.

What happened was that Rich got way stoned one night at the Blast right after Halloween and went back with Mary to her mom's house in Pawtucket. Mary says they started to fight over some petty disagreement and he got nasty, telling her she was nothing but a scrawny little wretched dyke fag hag. She told us it was only because Rich was so tight that he acted like that. He never was so mean as that as long as she could remember. There were times he might act like she was ignorant, like she bugged him some, but she figured all people got impatient with each other eventually, especially since they hung out together all the time. Anyways, Rich was loud and raging to the point of busting things up. Mary told him to get the hell out and he started bawling, kind of like howling, she said. Tears began to fall and he clung to his knees by the door, weaker than anybody she says she had ever seen, except her mom the day her dad split. This got Mary pretty scared so she told Rich to stay, but he kept saying no, no, and she was saying yes, yes, it was okay, till he finally got up and bolted out the door, down the stairs, out into the empty Pawtucket night street.

Mary tried to call Rich on the phone all night, but he never came home, and not the next day or the day after that. When she got him at last on the fourth day, he told her how he decided to walk off the weirdness after their fight, and he was almost home when the cops picked him up outside City Hall. A lot of fags hang around there late at night and the cops figured Rich was one of them and kept on calling him faggot and punk as they drove him out to India Point Park by the water over in the Portuguese neighborhood. They beat hell out of him.

Mary told us this one night at the Blast after there had been no sign of her or Rich for about three weeks. She said Rich spent three nights in the hospital and then he was afraid to leave home. He told Mary not to visit. She said he was sorry for going off that night and the reason he did was not so much that he was high or tight as he was just a coward and a fag, which everybody knew just looking at him. And he said him and Mary should just face facts and give up on going out. He even told her that he knew me and Sully thought he was a fag and we were right, and we should hardly feel bad for seeing the truth he was too chicken to admit. Sully and me felt sorry and bad about all this, and when Mary left we agreed we never should have called Rich "The Fag" so much and what a cool guy he was, and that we would miss his advice and of course all the drugs, too.

We saw Mary at the Blast all that winter. She had no more news from Rich. Sully would look at Mary and tell me how bad he wanted to do it with her. I told him to go ahead and go for it, but he never did. We stopped calling her a dyke behind her back. I guess because with no Rich there was no more sour grapes. I kept quiet about how I wanted to do it with Mary. Sully and me were best friends now, and he probably had an idea of what I thought about Mary, even though I never mentioned it. I liked her a hell of a lot. It was a kick to see her change the colors of her hair or come around with some new old rags that kept her looking like a hobo. Mary is the coolest girl hanging at the Blast but, of course, justice would have it that she goes to another school. Still, we can be down there and I just love to watch her go and crash all crazy into the spinning wheel of the pit, her arms gyrating and wild, crawling up over heads and shoulders onstage, first rolling on, then she skanks through the band with a face like this wicked four year old when she dives in the whirl of black and white and jeans. I can be all burned from the last jam and head beat up tired to the push and shove ring outside the spins and slams in the mosh, and she goes and takes over, better than me, cooler. And sometimes, she'll scream in my ear, Watch this! and go deck some backwoods skinhead or dive right in the face of some obnoxious Nazi punk.

One day I was home reading when Mary called to tell me how bored she was and I should come over. She said her mom got a bunch of new records from New York and we could listen to them together. It was so cold all week, I actually had to think about whether or not to face the outdoors. But her idea sounded good enough so I asked my mom for a few bucks and headed out into the North Pole.

The walk from the bus to Mary's house practically froze my ears, fingers, and toes for long-term preservation and I was glad to get inside. Mary made tea and I suggested we should raid her mom's liquor to put some rum in it so we did. We turned on the Japanese horror movie from the UHF channel out of Boston but kept the sound off to hear these great records. I told Mary her mom must be a swell lady to cop such excellent material. She said her mom knew everything good and a lot of weird, unknown shit, too. Her mom was going with some guy from New York who taught at RISD. He came to town in the middle of the week and then her mom would go to New York on weekends and check him out.

Mary explained that she and her mom were more like sisters. That made me wish my mom was more into what I like, instead of all her weirdo friends always talking about correct action and karma and bogus stuff like that. They always start blubbering on about how this thing I get into is negative and that I should say this wacky Buddhist chant, *namyorangyko* or something. As far as what I am into being negative, I never even claimed I was into anything at all. Besides, it seems pretty twisted to get all hung up on the right thing to do when every day the whole world is blowing up and dying right before our eyes. I just go to my room or split the house altogether when too many of her dippy freaks come around.

Then, me and Mary got on the subject of drugs. We both agreed drugs are the best way to expand the mind, wishing there was some way to get morphine or heroin or opium so we could try that like Lou Reed and Jim Carroll and Edgar Allen Poe used to do. That led us to planning a trip to New York, where you can get anything you want anytime, which somehow got us on the sex topic. Mary told me about her first girlfriend, this black chick from her school. She said they met walking home one day and this girl invited Mary to her house. She got Mary in the bedroom to look at this photo album and the next thing was they were making out. She went down on Mary, which I guess was freaky at first, but Mary said she got to really like it and she even did it back. She said this went on about six months but this other girl played these games and stood Mary up a lot. Mary really liked her and she said they never really broke up, they just sort of drifted apart.

Of course, now Mary asked me if I ever did it with boys, and I felt the sweat under my arms and my body get hot and I lied. I was hoping Rich had kept his mouth shut but naturally, he had told her everything. She said it was okay. She liked me, she said. Then she kissed me and unzipped my pants and started playing with it so that before I knew why, we were naked and I was blushing because I finally lost my virginity to a girl. Mary was super nice the whole time and kept asking was I okay and I said yes, or if I was nervous and I said no and she giggled. I tried to get on top to do it like missionaries, but she ended up on top of me and I did not last very long at all. I was totally embarrassed but she kept on kissing me lots, telling me I was a beautiful boy, and she moaned so much and loud enough that I got scared and wondered if I hurt her. It was a neat thing with Mary, not like Rich and Noel. I guess I had thought a lot about it instead of it just happening, even though I never believed it would, and it did sort of just happen. But it was cool. We held close a while as the record ended and the Japanese dragon movie turned into kung fu.

When we got up, Mary heated a pot of chili her mom left on the stove. We watched *Apocalypse Now* on cable, eating a few bowls of chili, a bag of Fritos, and some more rum. When the movie ended, we went to the Blast in a delirious head, making noises and faces at each other, dancing and skipping or walking too slow and too fast through the cold, empty winter night. We just leaned on each other that night, all quiet for a long time, then talking excitedly like we never did before between the rudies and hellacious rock—Bad Brains was in town—sneaking the softest kisses in the shadows.

One of the first spring days, when all the people are into this big phony smiley culture everywhere you go—pastel and white and Ray-Bans and automatic cameras in Providence, for Christ's sake—me and Mary headed for the park after school and thankfully, it wasn't too crowded, just a bunch of greasers in their mondo-mobiles over by the zoo. Sully was waiting over by Roger's big empty famous yellow house and lit up a zombie joint that only started to hit us fifteen minutes after we complained it was beat. Right as I started to feel burnt, here comes Rich in smelly black leather with no shirt on and he sits by Mary. He was smoking a joint he handed to her and asked if we wanted to cop some acid. Right away he pulled out this pistol that scared shit out of us, but we stayed cool like they say to do if a dog is after you and for a minute I wondered if it was real, too chicken to ask. He pulled the clip out to look in the hold and then down the barrel before dropping in two bullets and shoving it back in. I was amazed at how huge and black and shiny it was, like some movie piece, and the bullets had these ugly pointed ends I would not want to be in front of for anything. Rich went on about the acid, how good it was, said he just took thirteen hits. Then he offered some to us free since his money was taken care of. "I live on this shit and it's damn good for ya. Been takin' it every day for a month now and it's the best shit in the world." He raised his eyebrows, waiting for our answer. We shook our heads, no, like our mouths were glued by the paste the reefer made of our spit.

Rich was oblivious to our answer, just rubbing at the gun with a rag like he thought it was some magic lamp with a genie inside it waiting for his command. Mary and I were not holding hands and we shimmied our thighs apart to make it seem like we were not making out as much as we were. It seemed like forever we sat in the too quiet shadows of Roger Williams' big old house there in the park. I was tempted to ask Rich for some acid, not knowing what else to do, but my imagination was wild with all the horrible things he could do with the gun: rape us, kill us, all the terrorist torture you ever saw on the news or read in the papers or movies. So I figured the acid would only be worse and forgot about it.

Rich never said another thing until he stood up kind of mechanical, like one of those toys in that scientist's shop at the end of that movie about the replicant hunter. He stuck the gun in his jacket and walked down the hill, complaining what a bunch of little kids we were. When he was a good way, he stopped to look back like he left something. "Come on!" he yelled. We just sat there. He walked all the way back to us and stood all hazy a minute and then stared right at me. "Fuck you if I am a faggot, motherfucker." He was quiet for a couple minutes, just standing there like he liked making us all nervous and then he said, "You know my name, look up my number." That was when he left for good. We felt all ashamed and said nothing until I decided to joke about how hard Rich was tripping, saying he was tripping so hard he would fall up instead of down if he tripped on something else. We were stoned and dead anxious to forget what just went down, so my not very funny joke got us laughing real easy.

At first, me and Mary agreed this gun was Rich's way of scaring us, letting us know he was not so keen on us going out. We talked about breaking up for a while or not seeing each other so much or at least hiding out, but we decided there was nothing to do if Rich wanted to kill us. It would be chicken to call the cops, since even though Rich was acting crazy, he was still a cool guy, and especially not after what the pigs already did to him. I think me and Mary had a little bit of a death wish, too. Or the idea of going on with normal life had this extra tension, like all of a sudden now we were big Spanish dictators or mercenaries or something.

It only took a couple more times seeing him to let us know Rich was not pissed at us at all, or if he was, we were not his major problem. Rich had obviously gone a little whacked in the head. He came around to lecture us on how evil people were, how kids used to pound on him, burn him with cigarettes and matches, kick him down stairs, shove him in a Dumpster or toilets. There was this huge list of all the ways Rich was messed with right up until dropping out of school a month before graduation. He said he hated society because society hated him, so there was no point in graduating. If all the assholes thought one month of school made such a big difference, they were stupid and he did not need them to begin with. He hated politicians and big businesses and society. He kept saying everyone was a hypocrite, even him. He made all these speeches to us sitting hunched over the gun, staring at it, polishing it, spitting on it or on the ground at his feet. Sometimes he would spare us the speeches and just sit there muttering, "Fuckers, they won't fuck me." Just like that, over and over.

I was in the school cafeteria on another of those golden happy joy-joy days when everybody acts like the Pepsi company is paying people major bucks to smile. Right outside the window, the prom king and queen are making out like the Breakfast Club Star Search finals, when I see Rich walking over to the plaza with his gun. I doubt most people saw the gun at first, but by now I had a habit of looking for it whenever Rich came around. He usually had it, too. Of course, that was always at the park and he never came around the school. There was no reason for him to be there.

Rich came right into the cafeteria, pointing his gun at the old man security guard and a couple of teachers standing by the entrance. Everyone backed away slow with their hands up. No one screamed, but there were gasps and some kids made it out of the room. Most of us stood around and watched Rich pacing with his right arm out and the pistol tight in his fist. He pointed it at people, but he never pulled the trigger. Once, Rich let the gun brush through Cindy Hunt's white hair and she went stiff as a board. Some people said later she shit in her pants, and I wouldn't blame her. It was then Rich stopped to polish the gun a second, but only a second. He started pointing it at people's heads now, yelling out, "Fag? Who's a fag?!" His eyes started blinking all wild-like and his face was tight so he looked mad as hell. This only went on maybe a few minutes like they would never end, and then the old man security guard got out his gun, like remembering his job, and he followed Rich around the room. He kept aim on Rich but never fired, since I guess he was afraid it might ricochet or something, but he sure looked like he wanted to be a hero and do it.

It was not long before Rich sat down and, when he did, he put that pistol smack at the center of his own forehead. At the top of his lungs, he screamed out, "BANG! BANG! You're dead! Fifty bullets in your head!" And then he started in this nutty laugh. He let his arm drop so the gun rested in his open palm on the table. That was when all the last of the kids started leaving. A lot of us were slow about it and I hung back way longer than just about anybody else, even though it was not on my mind to help out at the time. I was fascinated like the rest, and probably a little relieved to be out of there.

Rich kept the security guard away until the cops came in full force, like fifty of them with shotguns and rifles and nightsticks and bullet-proof vests and walkie-talkies and some of them had on riot helmets and some others were wearing hats from that old SWAT team show. They got Rich surrounded easy, and he kept turning round and round with one hand on the gun and the other on his wrist, the way he must have seen in *Dirty Harry*, never pulling the trigger and mumbling something no one could understand. And then, Rich got all contorted in his face and his body and started singing this song:

Well, I asked a young policeman
If he'd only lock me up for the night
Well, I had pigs in the barnyard
Some o' them, they're all right
Then he fucked me with his truncheon
And his helmet was way too tight.

And then he started yelling the refrain, absolutely batshit, "Wait'll I get my cock sucked! Wait'll I get my ass fucked! I ain't got no money, but I know where to put it every time!" I doubt the cops were able to appreciate this little bit of Rolling Stones trivia, and a bunch of them rushed Rich and threw him on the ground as he got out the last words, "I'm a lonesome schoolboy in your town." We all heard his head smack the floor and there was this big weird sigh when it did, and then they cuffed Rich and beat him wicked bloody and carried him off to jail.

Sully was in his class during that lunch period and even though I told him what happened after he heard the rumors flying around, we never really talked about what it all means. I guess the reason you have a best friend is so there can be somebody you can avoid talking to about some things and still understand each other. As soon as I got home, I called Mary to fill her in. Later on, I went to her house from where I called my mom and lied to her that I was staying over at Sully's. After a major phone battle, she gave in and I ended up in front of the tube with Mary and a pizza. Sully came by and we hit the rum, but he wanted to make the Blast before closing, so he split around ten. It was a jittery, nervy night, the three of us sitting there real quiet, like waiting in the emergency room for some mangled friend.

None of us knows whether Rich will get a trial or be put in the crazy house or what. I keep avoiding the gossip at school, but I sometimes overhear things. All of it is usually a pointless crock of predictable idiocy from your hopeless high school needlebrains. Every now and then, some total no-mind will actually come up to ask if my girlfriend didn't used to screw that zany faggot who came to the lunchroom, and some of them even say they heard I was sucking his cock, too. I just tell them to fuck the hell off and leave it at that, otherwise I would end up in fights all day long. I just hope people are more intelligent when I leave this dump.

It's the first time you've ever littered at the beach.

That and the beer make you feel

powerful and old. (Zwahlen, page 27)

Postcolonial Fat Man

Chad McCracken

1. Tamale Plate

Up late, hungover, behind on grading,
behind on reading, on writing, hiding
from professors, coughing, flu-like symptoms,
credit cards maxed, unable to think, weeks,
months, years tearing past you, your twenties gone,
pissed away in a blur, "Sometimes I think
you're an idiot," your advisor says
off-handedly, a real monsoon of crap,
all pushed aside for a second while you
peel the greasy corn husks open, and eat.

2. Star of Siam

How many hostile mornings—long commutes
through slush, partners screaming "Where's my brief?"—eyes
clogged with prediabetic haze, your head in
pain—voice mail, e-mail stacking up, frantic
clients, hours slipping behind—how many
such days wiped half clean by an early lunch
at Star of Siam, pretty waitresses
knowing what you want, bringing out Thai iced
coffee, chicken salad, without a word?

Second Grade

Chad McCracken

Squanto loomed as large as Lincoln
in the histories of the day:
befriended the hapless Pilgrims;
taught them to farm—to sow dead fish
along with seeds (to fertilize
the soil); traveled to England; was
fêted; met the King; then returned
to find his tribesmen dead. Smallpox,
probably, or measles, Miss Krill
said. Next came the tale of Jenner,
of smallpox vaccine: "He made it
from cowpox that a milkmaid had.
Vaccines make you a little sick.
Then your antibodies in
your blood get stronger and can kill
the worse disease, like smallpox, but
the year when he made it was too
late to save Squanto's family
and all his friends, his Indian
ones not his Pilgrim ones." Or so
you wrote. One hundred, A plus.
Also important were the bush
pilots, and before them, the sled dogs:
rushing diphtheria serum
to Nome, always to Nome, it seemed.
Diphtheria ran wild in Nome.
Diphtheria is like the mumps,

your friend Kim told you, but she was
sometimes wrong. She was always in
trouble: Miss Krill caught her peeing
in the boys' bathroom once, in front
of boys. How come Miss Krill can go
in there, Scott whispered, she's a girl
herself, and then he said, that's how
a girl gets pregnant, you know, she
pees on a boy's thing and then he
pees on hers. You shook your head: it
seemed too outlandish. But Scott swore
it was true. So why didn't Kim get
pregnant—or expecting like your
mother said to say—why isn't Kim
expecting then, you asked him. He
wasn't sure. There was nothing about
pee in the World Book when you tried
to look it up. That afternoon
you drew a drawing of Squanto
crying, walking through some empty
woods, searching all over for his
friends. You drew in the sunset and
then two small owls to watch him look.
Scott drew a milkmaid with cowpox
sores, pus oozing from them. Miss Krill
gave Scott a D and you an A.
Then everyone traced hand turkeys.

. . . the fact was that all this brown beef, veined with fat, rich in violet-gold reflections under the low chandelier, that mountain whose color and steamy humidity reminded me of hot and secret bodily parts, that tremulous mass of meat aroused in me a mixture of repugnance and greed, because of which I continued to eat of it with a growing sense of nausea that was ready to overcome me, and I thought to myself, the butcher's emporium, the chopping block, the bed, arousing in me bestial images of abattoirs, of fresh blood, of sheep, slaughtered Minotaurs, and I started to murmur flesh, sacrificial victim, flayed alive, mutilation, Calvary, and I felt sad with a cosmic sadness, irremediable, the waves of paprika set my hair on fire, I was overtaken by an uncontrollable trembling of the hands, my eyes wept, I sweated blood, I was on the cross, my hands transfixed by huge rusty nails, on my head the crown of thorns, until everything went black and I fainted, they told me later, my face in the plate of tepid braised beef, my forehead, hair and nose in the gravy, brown, thick, and fat. (Longo, page 135)

Zach Harris

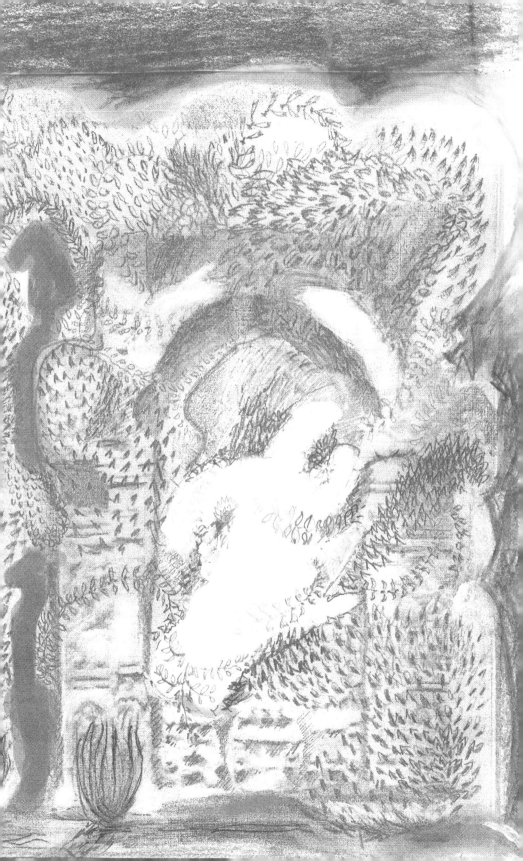

Still Life with Woodpecker

Joshua Beckman and Matthew Rohrer

The day before yesterday I felt frisky and set myself several tasks. The first was to bring several birdhouses inside and set them up like they were useful. By afternoon the birdhouses were arranged with the rest of my belongings. The second task I put into the drawer. The next task involved incredible dexterity and snaring of woodpeckers with dental floss which had been treated with oil. This turned ugly. Woodpeckers have traditionally been free. They fight and fight, love and fight and always always in their absolutely free ways. Sewing the miniaturized straightjackets I rethought the plan. Clearly this afternoon's new flavor is intoxicating and diverting me toward something alcoholic and fruity. Sipping and reflecting, I decided that the birds could be. Once this decision was made everything became brighter and I stretched my hamstrings and jogged out to the mailbox. There I discovered this: Dear Whoever, You have infringed upon my world. Now the time approaches for divine retribution and that specialty of mine known worldwide as the pinch of doom will come! Alarmed, I left this letter and jogged on. The experience of watching pornography as meta-textual artistic folderol came easily to me while jogging. Everyone I passed looked pornographic. Stopping in to get recharged, I asked four people this question, "How ugly is this?" They screamed about their woodpeckers and then I realized what destiny had meant for me. I was amazing as a child but now I have merely taken root. This isn't at the heart of things but it's somewhat responsible for everything that would become apparent later. Flying overhead were woodpeckers. They didn't notice me. After all, my tasks were illusory. Nothing except drinking and stretching and wondering about the birds.

The Book of Houseplants

Joshua Beckman and Matthew Rohrer

Great nests dried today will burn brightly tomorrow. Birds often land several times before they settle into a routine. Janet tersely explained to her guests that the houseplants had delicate constitutions and they needed two hours of absolute quiet. Beginning with now. The guests looked around anxiously for to leave but Janet was ahead of them and locked eyes and raised hell without speaking. They cowered. Houseplants do not get out, she said softly but, they learn by absorbing. But everyone listened while she quizzed. The afternoon lengthened. Crickets in cages began lamenting. Two beehives that produced from roses' friends' gardens were cackling outside. The houseplants know how. They take lessons in evil from Janet and apply them to their surroundings. The air choked by pollen grew morbid and the guests inwardly signed their wills. Janet had houseplants. She knew they could easily grow to be her if she let down her guard. Her *Time* magazine fluttered away. No one needs guests if their subscriptions continue. Read about her in this issue.

Why?

Ava Woychuk-Mlinac

LOUD CLAPPING,
soft talking,
WHY?

When his kids ask why they don't have a new car he says, "these cars were new once and now and they are experienced." (Harrison, page 21)

Seven Spells

Dawn Raffel

1.

HUNGRY. CRASH DIET. HIT THE FLOOR IN THE HIGH SCHOOL corridor and get sent home. I wasn't out more than a minute they say, insist to me. I thought I was moving, maybe jigging uncontrollably. I still have the scar on my chin.

2.

Lab class. It's called "Pests, Parasites, and Man"—an improbable freshman science class for humanities students, kids who wouldn't stand a chance in Physics 101. It's, by the way, the only class that hadn't been closed out at registration. The lab is suffocating. Our teaching assistant, in lieu of instruction, has taken to showing us graphic film footage of infectious diseases. We've had rocky mountain fever and whatever the thing is you get from a cat that's dangerous when you're pregnant—toxoplasmosis. Today's diseases are amoebic dysentery followed by cholera. We are watching barely living skeletons expel diarrhea. There can't be any hope—by now, at the time of our viewing, they must surely be dead—yet the volunteer medics are bucketing vomit, looking with a needle for a vein. During an intubation into the neck on a patient whose veins appear to have collapsed, I fall off my lab stool and hit the concrete floor head first. I don't know where I am—or where I was—but I have been here before. Someone turns the lights on. The teaching assistant stops the film; it sputters off. He hadn't watched it first, he concedes, before showing it to us. Perhaps, he says, this one was a bit too . . . he's searching for a word. Early, he says—class is let out early.

Everyone, it seems, is heading for the lakefill, our hard shore built of what has been cast off.

Back at my dorm, I look in the bathroom mirror at the gash across my forehead, the bird's egg (or is it goose?) that's starting to form. I try to do the crossword puzzle that someone has taped, along with a pencil stub on a string, to the door of a stall. My eyes hurt, so I go to my room and lie down. My roommate is elsewhere, as ever; when her parents call, as they do, I tell them she's just down the hall, in the shower, indisposed. "Dinner time," my friend says, entering while knocking. When I tell her I don't want to eat, she makes me put my shoes on to walk to the infirmary. I think this is a terrible idea.

The person who examines me says he is an "extern" and looks to me to be about my age. He shines in my eyes and listens through his stethoscope, then says he has concluded I don't have a concussion— "But," he says. But, but, but. "Do you know you have a heart murmur?" he says. He won't let me go home. When I wake up, my mother is there. "You look upset," I say. She's looking in her purse. She keeps Kleenex in her purse. Someone, she says, from the infirmary called her and told her I had a concussion. "How could you—?" she says.

"Your father," she says, over club sandwiches, no middle slice. Then we go to a real doctor, who fails to find anything going on with my heart. "Concussion?" he says. "Possible." What I have are two black eyes, so we swing by the drugstore that cashes checks and stock up on Erase before my mother leaves.

The gash is scabbing over. My nose is badly swollen. People ask me whether I've been in an accident—meaning, with a car. My sweet, elderly Russian teacher tells me it's okay for me to miss the last week of class before Thanksgiving. She tells me to go home, then says something inflected that I can't understand. Walking around with pods of mismatched makeup under my eyes, I seem to make people wary. When my report card comes at the end of the term, I see that I've gotten an A in "Pests, Parasites, and Man."

3.

Blood test. I stand up, then fall down. The nurse can't find a pulse at first and panics. I tell her I must have one, then lie back down.

4.

Sugar Pops—dinner—in the seventh-floor walkup I share with a roommate on Thompson Street, so small that it never takes more than one ring to answer the phone (except I rarely do), before heading out with girls I know—transplanted Midwesterners, girls in search of something, or anything, too easy to impress—to a place in Soho. We can't afford to drink, but someone always pays for us—at least, that's what we tell ourselves. I'm wearing a delicate lavender dress that's somehow ridiculous the minute we walk in the door. It's a cavernous place, six deep to the bar. This time I sit on the floor before losing consciousness. When I come to on the sidewalk, the bouncer who carried me out wants my friends to tell him what I took. I think I've been out for hours; it feels like a hole in the night. "You'd better tell the truth," he says. Cab home—can't afford it. I never wear the dress again.

5.

Eight months gone, I make a last trip home to see my mother, my father, places I grew up. Did I mention my father? He lives way down the lake. I want everything to be the way it was before I left.

The baby is kicking; perhaps he's upside down.

Leaving again, it's an hour to the airport in Milwaukee, so my father and I are up and out before the sun. He says he doesn't mind, but he's dark around the eyes. His hands are liver spotted on the wheel. My father likes to talk about astronomy and molecules, the nature of the firmament, small product manufacturing (he's patented a chair designed to trigger certain brain waves), Latin music, ballroom dancing, aeronautics, aging. "I believe," he says, "we could extend the human life span, maybe by at least one hundred years." He is eating in the car—a banana, pills. "Want some?" he says. I miss him already.

The plane reeks of sauce. The food cart is coming . . . and two women are wavering above me with an oxygen tank. They're flight attendants, uniformed. One says I had a seizure. "You made a noise," she says. The other says I need to eat right now, have this plastic tray of breakfast, which is orange juice—fine—and airline crêpes in cream. I eat a few bites and start vomiting profusely. I need a second bag, a third, can't make it down the aisle to the bathroom. There's nothing but fluid. The baby isn't kicking. The man from Racine in the seat next to mine, having given me his bag, is at a loss. "I'm sorry," I say. "I'm so sorry," I say. "Air traffic"—it's the flight attendant back again, the grave one—"The captain—" What is she saying? "Could you please get ahold of yourself?" she says.

Forty minutes early, we're at LaGuardia, as if there were a secret route through distance and time. Some people seem annoyed by time to kill. The paramedics take me off, cuff my arm. My blood pressure alarms them. "Look at this," says one to the other. "Will you look?" There are two of everyone today, it seems. They want to take me to Jamaica hospital; I insist on going to a pay phone (my dime). The paramedics make me sign a waiver stating that I'm knowingly ignoring their advice.

By the time I get to my doctor, twenty minutes later, the baby is active. We listen to the heartbeat. "You're fine," my doctor says. "Go home and eat starch." I call my husband, who goes out to buy the crackers.

When I call my dad, I say my flight arrived the better part of an hour early. "Really," he says. "That never happens to me."

6.

Labor room. Everyone is leaving. The nurse slips out, my doctor, who is pregnant (what a sight we must be!) takes a swollen ankle break, and my husband—we've done this before—is buying something for a headache. My father's parents, who are dead, come into the room together. Everything is fine with them. The baby is fine, fine, fine. I am very happy. A woman is screaming. Something is slapped on my face and I open my eyes and I'm under an oxygen mask. "Delivery!" the woman says. My husband's face appears. I'm lifted, heaved and wheeled. "Is there oxygen in there?" my doctor keeps asking. My grandparents—people are yelling at me. "Push! Push-push!" There's a whole crowd in here. Someone checks the plastic mask I'm pushing off my face. I feel the baby leaving me. They take away the baby. Then they bring the baby back, and then he looks at me and takes my breast, and then they take him away again.

I am on the phone, leaving messages for everyone. No one is home. Later a doctor enters my room and tells me not to worry, he's checked the baby over and the baby is fine. "Why wouldn't he be?" I ask. The doctor wants to know if I remember him—the whole team, with the crash cart. I shake my head no.

7.

Tetanus shot—preventative; why wait for a rusty nail? ("Do you know what lockjaw looks like?" my mother used to say.) I pay my co-pay and collapse. Women in the waiting room are swooning over me. It was quicker than I think, they say, of shorter duration, this blackout or spell. I thought that I was home, in a room that is gone, and also somehow in motion. The receptionist is speaking with a certain irritation. "Your patient—" she says to the intercom system. She makes me eat a cracker, two crackers from somewhere, left over from lunch. "I don't like this," my doctor says, reading a meter. She won't let me look. When she lets me stand, I can't make it to the door.

The doctor calls at night. She wants to talk to me; she is talking to me about things that end in "noma." I fire her.

I get worked up. Knock on wood. No noma, the endocrinologist says. He has a name for my condition, which I make him repeat. It escapes me again.

The babies have birthdays. My grandfather appears in a dream where he's carrying the body of a man I can't identify. My father sits down swiftly, surprisingly gracefully, witnesses say, while dancing, and never gets back up. When I call the house, I get his voice on the machine but the body is elsewhere, in storage, is ash.

There are no more spells. I am learning things, like when to keep my head down and the uses of salt.

The underbrush rustled apart for

two little pigs. They

were unusually hairy, primeval,

and cute. *(Smith, page 65)*

Snow Man

Katherine Hollander

I am making a man
of snow. Better
I am making a god

of snow. His attendants
will be white hares
and little white snails,

he will put his foot
prints on the land
with his arms around

tall white swans. Children
will leave blue bowls
of white custard on window

sills for him, but mothers
will bury the clean bones
of fowl in their door

yards to keep him away
from their children and men
will leave broken eggshells

on their doorsteps
to keep him away
from their wives. When

he comes to young maidens
he carries sheaves
of cold white lilies

like frozen bells,
their stems sharpened
to points, dazzles

them with his long thigh
bones, his curls
like a row of white shells

across his forehead.
Each year he is betrayed.
Girls choose human

loves and children take
the bowls from the sills and eat
the custard themselves. Eggs hatch,

chickens cluck in the yards, flicking
their brown feathers. The hares
shed their white coats

and orange muzzled ducks
with violet breasts pluck
little white snails from the mud.

Three Pieces of *Severance*

Robert Olen Butler

After careful study and due deliberation it is my opinion the head remains conscious for one minute and a half after decapitation.
　　　　—Dr. Dassy d'Estaing, 1883

In a heightened state of emotion, we speak at the rate of 160 words per minute.
　　　　—Dr. Emily Reasoner, *A Sourcebook of Speech*, 1975

Maximilien Robespierre
Lawyer and revolutionary,
guillotined by the Revolutionary Convention, 1794

my father is dressed immaculately his knee breeches his silk stockings his tailcoat my mother dead in the parlor her arms folded across her chest he leans against the far wall and I am trying to get my arms around Augustin and Charlotte and Henriette they seem like children to me now, my brother and my sisters, though I am myself only six years on this earth I try to hold them my arms straining and inadequate I know already the man leaning there is dead to us too and I am responsible and the door shuts hard the knocker clangs he has said nothing I follow quickly and strain at the door and he is gone his horse clatters away and he is gone the Bois de Boulogne is full of citizens dressed innocently in tricolor trousers and clogs and red caps I walk among them my hound at my side the summer daylight lingering and they look to me and I want to open my arms they are children and there are many who would harm them and I am in my room above the carpentry yard the sky incarnate with dawn my words prepared at last for the Convention and I dress in white silk stockings and knee breeches and floral waistcoat and black tailcoat and red cravat and my hair is powdered and on the cobbles a scaffold and the blade, dear father, for us all

Jacob
American slave,
beheaded by his owner, 1855

sowbelly frying in the first coming-up light I smell it being only a child my Sukey-mammy whisper me about how my own from-her-body mammy done been sold away but she still loves me the morning bell ringing on some other plantation far off Sukey-mammy singing *my way's cloudy go send them angels down* our own morning bell ringing and I am a strong-back man and the driver beats me bullwhip fire, now across my right side, now across my left, and another day he beats me, and another, my back always on fire, clearing some new part of the forest for corn and for cotton the chopping done and the grubbing and the log heaps piled and burning filling the night sky with flame and I know something burning in me and Sukey lying in the dirt the driver nudging her at the shoulder with his boot cause she tell a child how he have a soul of his own and that night I am rushing and my thumbs dig deep in the driver's throat and I lay a torch to a hayrick the sky going hot as a bullwhip lash behind me the hounds calling and I am running hard through corn row and forest and I am a child and I walk just a little ways from my Sukey to the window and I see the first fire of dawn and a bell is ringing far off somewhere

Alwi Shah
Yemeni executioner,
beheaded for a crime unrelated to his work, 1958

I hover down low and then I rise and a row of heads sits before me on a stone wall ear-to-ear arrayed beyond my sight to either side I face them and their eyes turn to me the stirring of feet and all about me now a jumbled huddling-in of bodies naked and battered with bones cracked and bulging knots and blooms of bruise and crusted lappings of blood, how I loved you all, loved righteously snapping the cords of all your lives, and so you come to taunt me but praise Allah I have done his holy work and I took as his sign the trill of sweetness that came upon me in this my work and now I turn and look into the bulging stone-shattered face of Haleema Alsakkaf an adultering woman and she holds in her right hand the head of Akram Alshami her lover who like the others moves his eyes to me and I say *praise Allah you have paid righteously* and she says *praise Allah who we call the one god and who loves his creatures we are sent as you knew us but we are restored in heaven* and I know suddenly that my head hangs in her left hand and I cry *praise Allah he will have mercy on me also* and she says *the mercy of god seeks sinful love before righteous hatred* and I wait for my head to fall

Goodbye, Blue Thunder

James C. Strouse

EVERYONE IN THE HOUSE WAS OUT OF WORK AND UNHAPPY except for Mom. Mom was in work and unhappy. She had two jobs, a nine to five at the Danner's Five and Dime and a weekend shift working nights at Bobby Jo's Party Shoppe. Dad and my brother spent all their time trying to figure out the best way to utilize Mom's earnings. They usually did this over continual rounds of tap stout at the Dew Drop Inn downtown. Both had plenty of ideas but no initiative. Each night they'd come home exhausted by the possibilities, eat dinner, then pass out in front of the TV, a Stroh's tallboy at their feet and Mom's glassy eyes on their dumb slumbering faces.

Once asleep, Mom would go to her bedroom and work on a letter to her friend, Cindy Kyle. Cindy had moved to Florida with her husband, Duke, a year ago and Mom had been saving for a trip down to visit ever since. It was a small pathetic thing to save for, seeing as Florida was mainly just a long hot place old people went to die and Cindy never really seemed to like Mom that much anyway. But I guess everybody needs a dream.

My dream was no less than full-blown nonstop-getting-my-cock-sucked rock stardom. My bandmates, Steve, Jon D. and me had all just graduated high school and were now free and ready to pursue music full-time. We'd meet in my neighbor's shed every night at midnight. Split the warm Stroh's Dad and brother didn't finish. Talk band names.

Jon D. liked to suggest animals.

"What about the Rabbits?" he said.

"Or the Fucking Rabbits," said Steve. Steve was a round kid with a fat neck and a little head. I wondered if his blood had trouble pumping up his chubby throat to his brain. The boy was incredibly dim. But he was the only guy in the band who actually had an instrument. A Fender bass. And he knew how to play it, too.

"Who are we supposed to be fucking?" said Jon D.

"Everyone," said Steve. He guzzled the last of our Stroh's, then looked at me for approval.

I shook my head, no.

"Rabbits fuck other rabbits," said Jon D. "People would think we fuck each other."

"Yeah," said Steve. He looked down at his bass and slapped its strings.

"Whatever we choose, it should be something classic," I said.

Jon D. sneered. "We could call ourselves the Stones," he said.

"I like that," said Steve.

"It's taken, dip-shit," said Jon D. "And you can't *pick* a classic name. That's something it becomes."

Jon D. and I both considered ourselves the band's leader. We constantly battled over small points like this.

I argued with Jon D. that his thinking was limited.

Jon D. argued that everyone's thinking was limited and the only thing that mattered was whether or not you knew your limits.

Steve suggested we call ourselves the Shitty Limits.

Jon D. and I both told him to shut up. Then we started my neighbor's riding lawn mower and drove it over our empty tallboys, crushing them flat as tin foil before splitting up and going to bed.

Mornings Mom and I ate breakfast together. Commiserated over the past day's defeats. Prepared for their reoccurrence.

"You father's stopped touching me," said Mom, with a heap of instant oatmeal in her mouth.

"Well, that's good," I said.

"No," she said.

"Oh," I said. "Can I get a guitar?"

"Sure," said Mom.

"I think they're like a hundred dollars."

"Start working."

"I can't work until I have the guitar."

"Yes you can," said Mom.

"Music is a job," I told her.

Mom nodded. She was careful never to squelch hope of any kind in the house.

"I need it before Jon D. gets one."

"We'll see," she said.

"Or I'll have to play drums."

"We don't want that," said Mom.

"No, we don't," I said. Because the only way I could hope to lead the band as a drummer was if I also sang. And the precedents for singing drummers in music were not inspiring. They all strained too hard to keep a beat as they sang. It made everyone I'd ever seen look constipated and graceless.

"Jon D. would lead the band for sure," I said.

"I thought you liked Jon," said Mom.

"I do," I said. "He just lacks vision."

"Oh," said Mom.

"I'm afraid he'd bend to the will of any mid-level studio exec just to get our music released."

"I hadn't realized you boys had made any music," said Mom.

"We haven't," I said. "But it's important to think this stuff out first."

"Sure." Mom smiled and looked out the window at our sick elm in the front lawn.

I sat and schemed over the band's trajectory. Sucked milk from a bowl. Burped into my mouth.

I believed artistic integrity led to the best twat and wanted to take the band in that direction. Any group could luck upon popularity with a few chords and a good stylist. But if that was all they had, they'd be doomed to recede into club-land obscurity after a couple of years, scoring, at best, some middle-aged biker moms with flat asses and bad attitudes after their shows. Visionaries, on the other hand, enjoyed prime pussy throughout their entire careers. Even if they were misshapen little dorks with bad teeth and thick glasses. It didn't matter what you looked like. If fans honestly believed you made something true and lasting, they'd let you fuck them raw until you died.

"Poor tree," said Mom.

"Uh-huh," I said, as I sat thinking of girls.

"Your father should do something."

Girls touching themselves. Girls touching themselves as they touched other girls. Girls touching themselves as they touched other girls touching me. Girls watching. Waiting. Videotaping.

"I'm tired of watching it die," she said.

"Yeah," I said. "What about the guitar?"

"I don't know, Julian," said Mom. "I think we should ask your father." I guess Mom hoped this suggestion would delay the matter for a couple of days. Give her a chance to think about it. Maybe buy a cheap-ass one behind my back with which to surprise-slash-disappoint me. But unlike her, I had no qualms destroying other's hopes, especially if they were in opposition to my own.

I brought up the guitar with Dad later that night, at dinner.

"Hey, Dad," I said.

Dad didn't respond. He sat staring at the charred salmon patties on his plate like he was trying to lift them with his mind. He and my brother, Joel, had both come home late from the Dew Drop, beer-dazed and ashamed. A perfect time to ask the old man for something.

"Dad?"

"Huh?" he said.

"Hi."

"Oh," he said. "Hey."

Mom watched, scraped a path with her fork through her half-finished plate of fish cakes and potato hash. Joel sat with his head bent, leaned his weight slightly to pass gas as he ate.

"How's it going?" I said.

"Good," said Dad.

"Good," I said.

Mom sighed, looked out the window. It was night and there was nothing to see but the dark outline of our diseased elm.

Dad smiled. Stuck his fork in a salmon patty. He was once a handsome man. But all his fine features had fizzed out from drinking. Now his stomach was severely bloated, which made him look like he was wearing a heavy coat-vest under his clothes. His green eyes were always pink at the rims. And his lips were dry and withered as a sun-rotted apple.

"Has Mom told you about the band I started with Jon D.?" I said.

"Who's Jon D.?" said Dad.

"A friend," I said.

Dad looked pained.

"My best friend, since middle school," I said.

He turned to Mom.

"The Duesler boy," she said.

"That kid?" said Dad.

"Yeah," I said.

"What are you doing with him?" he said.

"Starting a band," I said.

My brother sniffed, forced a laugh, and started coughing. Joel was a thirty-year-old man who had never lived apart from Mom and Dad for longer than a month. He hated me for being younger, smarter, and better looking. Whereas I had Dad's emerald eyes and high cheekbones, Joel had the lips and tits of Mom. Whereas I had the promise of a man just starting out, Joel had the tired resignation of a long-standing failure. And whereas I still believed in my own potential, Joel had given up believing in much besides other people's inevitable doom. He rooted for my downfall. Seeing me as broken and disappointed as him was his dream.

"You play an instrument?" said Dad.

"I want to play guitar," I said.

"Sounds loud," said Dad.

"It's quieter than drums," I said.

"What isn't?" said Dad.

My brother smiled and bared his crooked underbite at me.

"Mom and I were talking about getting me one," I said.

"A drum?" said Dad.

"Guitar," I said.

"Oh," he said. "You have a bicycle, Julian?"

"Yes," I said, afraid Dad was going to make some lame point about being thankful for what you got. Tell me to forget the guitar.

"Still ride it?" he said.

"Sometimes," I said.

Dad reached into his pocket and passed me a damp beer coaster folded over in a half moon. "Don't tell that Duesler kid about this," he said.

I studied the coaster. The printed side had a picture of a couple holding hands on a beach at sunset. On the other side was a crudely rendered drawing of what looked like a backward lowercase h with the words "bike frames" written under it.

"Patio chairs," said Dad. "Made from bike frames."

"Oh," I said. Summer always inspired Dad with new ideas for lawn furniture.

"Your brother drew the prototype."

"That's great," I said to Dad. "What do you think about the guitar?"

Dad took back the coaster. Set it beside Mom's plate. "What does your mom think?" said Dad.

"She thought we should ask you."

Mom didn't look at the drawing on the coaster. She had lost interest in Dad's ideas years ago.

"Huh," he said. "That's funny."

"Yeah," I said, looking at Mom.

She placed her ice water on Dad's coaster, listening intently with her head turned down. "So, what do you think?" I said. "About the guitar?"

"I think your mother just didn't want to tell you no."

"Oh," I said. I knew he was right.

"But neither do I," said Dad.

"Then don't," I said.

"How much do they cost?" he said.

"I think about a hundred dollars," I said.

"Well, find out for sure," said Dad.

Oh, what a good-hearted lovable drunk Father could be. Teasing promises on Mother's dime. I worshiped him during these little moments. Of course, I'd be lucky to get him to remember anything the next day.

I told Steve the good news that night at our band meeting, a session that Jon D. had rudely decided to skip without notifying either one of us.

"So, I think I'm finally getting an ax," I said, sitting on my neighbor's mower.

"Why?" said Steve.

"To play," I said.

"Play what?"

"Guitar."

"With an ax?"

I shook my head and swiped his Stroh's. Finished it for him.

"Hey," he said. "That one was mine."

"Was," I said.

"Where's Jon D.?" said Steve.

"I don't know," I said. "He can't keep pulling shit like this, though."

"Like what?" said Steve.

"Like not showing up to rehearsals."

"We never rehearse anything," said Steve.

"That's a bad attitude to take," I said.

"But it's true," he said.

"What's true is that Jon D.'s not as committed to this as we are."

Steve shrugged.

"Or else he'd be here, wouldn't he?"

"I guess," said Steve.

"I'm not going to tolerate this shit when I get my guitar," I said.

"You're getting a guitar?" asked Steve.

"Yes, dip-shit."

"Oh." Steve looked around the shed. Scratched his chest. Picked up my neighbor's gas can.

"How do you get high with this stuff?" he asked.

"I don't know," I said, mildly buzzed and highly annoyed. "I think you drink it."

"For real?"

"No, Steve, for fake."

"Huh," he said.

"I'm going to bed," I said.

"Okay," said Steve.

I left the shed with him holding the red metal gas can like some expensive thing that he might want to buy someday. Got in bed. Fondled myself.

The next day I went down to the Cromwell pawnshop to check out guitars. They had five. Three acoustic and two electric. All but one of them was under a hundred dollars. The one I wanted. A bad ass-looking V-shaped thing with an azure-glitter finish and the words "Blue Thunder" stenciled on it in black. As far as I was concerned, the guitar was the only thing in the store. It was beautiful. It converted me instantly. I had faith in the thing, the type my mother claimed to have in Jesus. But instead of forgiving my sins, I believed Blue Thunder was going to absolve me of sin for the things I'd failed to do. The effort I never put forth in school. The colleges I never got into. The girls I never took out. Sex I never had. Purpose never felt. I'd use Blue Thunder to shred all those things away. Grind my malaise into avant-garde music with hummable melodies. Get laid and respected for it. Then share my anguished and lethargic past in candid interviews with high-profile rock journalists. Tell them how no one ever expected me to amount to much. How Dad drank and Joel farted as I worked out songs on Blue Thunder in my bedroom. Weep openly at the thought of myself at that time.

I asked a lady at the counter if I could see the guitar. She handed it to me like it was just another thing. I forgave her. Put the strap over my shoulder and walked to a mirror. It looked right as Christ on the cross in my hands.

"You're holding it wrong," said the lady behind the counter.

"What?" I said.

"Loosen the strap," she said. "It isn't supposed to be at your chest."

"I got it," I said.

"Be careful," she said.

"Yeah," I said. I loosened the strap and the guitar almost fell to the floor.

The lady took it back from me quickly. Said I could drop the thing all I wanted once I paid for it.

So, I went down the block to Danner's to talk to Mom about money. When I got there she was ringing up an old woman for a box of Dimetapp and a pair of sunglasses.

"Julian," said Mom with a big smile. She loved when I visited her at the store.

"Mom," I said looking at the Dimetapp woman. "I found a guitar but it's three hundred dollars."

"Oh," said Mom. She gave the old woman her receipt and closed the register.

"Is that too much?" I said. "I hope it's not too much."

"Julian," Mom said. She shook her head, no.

"How much *could* we afford?" I said.

"Not much."

"Why?" I said.

"Do you have to ask?"

"Because you're hoarding all our money for Florida?" I said.

Mom said nothing. She watched as the old woman inched out the store.

"I bet that trip costs more than three hundred dollars," I said.

"I've been saving for a year."

"That's kind of selfish of you, Mom."

"Don't say that," she said.

"It is," I said.

"That's not fair, Julian," said Mom.

"What's not fair?" I said and left the store with an affected sigh and exaggerated slouch.

That night neither Steve nor Jon D. showed up for rehearsal. So, I abandoned the shed and went to my bedroom with Dad and Joel's Stroh's. Slammed down both in under ten minutes as I sat on the floor and wrote ideas for song titles in a composition notebook I'd never used for senior chemistry. Every idea was a variation on the same theme:

Life Is Fucked

Fucking Life

Fucking Unfair Life

Fuck This Fucking Unfair Fucking Life

How Fucked am I (The Unentitled Song)

Fuck

Fuck

Fuck

Further down the page I wrote:

All I Want Is All I'll Never Have

(and) Goodbye, Blue Thunder, Goodbye

(and) Mom Is a Bitch, Mom's a Bitch

Bitch

Bitch

Selfish Bitch

Then I drew a pair of sagging tits with blood the color of black ink bleeding out the nipples and took a piss in one of my empty cans.

Mom saw the notebook the next morning when she came into my room to wake me for breakfast. It was open to the page of song titles. I was half awake and watched her pick it up and examine the page more closely. Her reaction was strange. She did not gasp or sigh. She didn't get hysterical or shake me awake, demanding an apology. All she did was quietly place the notebook back on the floor and gather my beer cans. She sniffed the one with my urine in it. When she realized what it was, she held it away, at arm's length, as she walked out of my room and closed the door behind her.

I decided not to join her for breakfast that morning. Instead, I went back to sleep and didn't wake up until I heard the sound of my brother's daily whale farts in the bathroom at noon. I waited for Dad and my brother to head off to the Dew Drop before leaving my room. Once they were gone, I went to the kitchen, fried an egg and gave Jon D. a call.

"We need to talk," I said. I made a concerned face as I waited for Jon D.'s response.

"No shit," he said.

"I feel like the band is falling apart."

"What are you talking about?" said Jon D.

"First you skip a rehearsal. Then Steve and you both skip one. I mean . . ."

"Steve's sick," he said.

"He can't call?" I said.

"He swallowed gasoline," said Jon.

"What?" I said.

"Dumb shit almost died."

"No," I said.

"Yes," said Jon D. "Says you told him to do it, too."

"Me?"

"What kind of dick are you, anyway?" said Jon.

"Look," I said.

"Shut up," he said.

"What do you want me to say?" I said.

"Just meet us in the shed tonight," he said.

"Us?" I said.

"There's a new guy," said Jon D. "He's got a kit that'd be perfect for Valvoline."

"Who's Valvoline?"

"It's our band name," said Jon D. "I let Steve pick it, since he almost bit it and everything. It's the type of gas he swallowed."

"Don't I get a say?"

"We can talk about that tonight," said Jon D., then he hung up the phone.

I could see where this was heading. I'd fucked up. Now Jon D. felt that he had complete control over the band and wasn't sure he needed me in it at all anymore. And the only way I could think to convince him otherwise was if I had Blue Thunder.

So, I called Florida. I rooted through my mother's things for the Kyles' number. Took a breath, dialed, hung up, dialed again.

"Hello," answered Cindy, the second time.

"Um," I said.

"Hello?"

"Hi. Cindy?"

"Yes?"

"It's Julian."

"Julian?"

"Julian Cripe. From Indiana."

"Oh," said Cindy.

"I was calling about my mom."

"Is there something wrong?" asked Cindy.

"Sort of," I said.

Cindy said nothing.

"It's just . . . I'm not sure she's going to have enough money to come visit you this summer."

"Visit me?"

"I know she's been planning this trip forever but . . ."

"What are you talking about?" said Cindy.

"My mom," I said. "Katherine."

"Katherine Cripe?"

"Yeah," I said.

"Is coming to Florida?"

"Well, I'm not sure." I said. "That's sort of why I was calling. To see if you could come up here instead."

"To see your mother?"

"Yeah."

"Are you kidding?" said Cindy.

"No," I said.

"I think you have the wrong number," said Cindy.

"You're Cindy Kyle, right?"

Nothing. A disconnect. I called again.

"Look," answered Cindy. "I don't know who this is. But you better stop calling."

"Uh," I said. "It's Julian Cripe."

"Why are you doing this?"

"Because my mom wants to see you."

"Please don't do this," said Cindy. And then she hung up again. It was my third hang up in a row. It seemed I couldn't even finish a simple phone call. A precedent for the rest of my efforts that day.

In the afternoon I took an hour-long half-shit on the toilet. After that, I went to my brother's room and flipped through his *Penthouse*, but I couldn't get my dick to fill with enough blood for more than one good jerk-off. I was so distracted and anxious that I couldn't even finish reading the Forum section, which usually enthralled me like nothing else in this world. Then, that night at dinner, I couldn't finish my food. A heaping plop of goulash served on our worn white porcelain plates.

"What's wrong?" asked Mom as I spooned through my stew.

I wanted to tell her but there was too much wrong for me to begin. What was wrong was that I had accidentally convinced dumb fat-necked Steve to drink gasoline. And as a result I'd probably get kicked out of the band. What was wrong was that Mom was going to waste all our money on a trip her best friend didn't even want her to make. And if I told her I'd be exposed as the greedy, backhanded shit that I was. But if I didn't Mom would still end up spent with grief and disappointment. Either way I wasn't going to get my guitar. And that, to me, was the biggest injustice of this all. What was wrong was that opportunity was passing me by. And if my life continued in this way, these days would not turn into sentimental fodder for interviews in music mags. Instead, these days would just become lost time. Gone.

Not even forgotten. Because I didn't even do enough to forget. I just existed, like a stone under a stone in the bottom of the ocean, which might be some ideal state to an idiot Buddhist but useless to me and my dingus.

"Nothing," I told Mom.

"You seem upset," she said.

Dad and Joel both looked at me.

"No," I said, afraid she was going to bring up the stuff she read in my notebook that morning.

"Something wrong?" said Dad.

I shook my head.

"What's wrong?" he asked Mom.

"I don't know," she said.

Joel rolled his eyes and sighed. Dad grinned. Mom looked out the window.

"Has he found a drum yet?" said Dad.

"Guitar," said Mom.

Dad faced me. "Well?" he said. "You find one?"

"No," I said.

"Where you looking?" he said.

"I sort of stopped," I said.

"You ought to look around here," he said.

"Uh-huh," I said. Mean drunken fuck.

"I'm serious," said Dad. "Have you looked in the closet?"

I stared at the old man searchingly. He just looked drunk as always. But Joel seemed more pissed off than usual, which made me think there might actually be something to Dad's question. I went to see.

Sometimes things work out exactly as you'd hoped they would. No, not sometimes. Actually, never. Things never work out exactly as you'd hoped. But there are times that come close. And for me, no one moment came as close to my hope of it as when I opened our coat closet and found Blue Thunder with a note attached that read:

For our favorite songs yet to be written.

You're our music.

Love,

Mom and Dad

And no moment came as far away from my hope of it as the one that occurred later that night in my neighbor's shed.

"What's that?" said Jon D. He stared at my guitar, which I wore self-consciously behind my back upon entering the shed.

"This?" I said, grabbing its neck and pulling it around. "It's my new guitar."

Jon D. turned to the new guy, a skinny kid with thin black hair and an angry face.

"What do you think?" said Jon D. to the kid.

"How's it play?" said the kid.

"Fine," I said.

"Where's the amp?" said Jon D.

"I don't have one of those yet."

"Shit," said the kid.

"Who is this?" I asked Jon.

"Darren," said the kid.

"His brother works a club up in Ft. Wayne," said Jon D. "He likes our band name."

"So," I said.

"Let me see that," said Darren. He grabbed for my guitar.

I backed away.

"Just let him see it," said Jon D.

"Be careful," I said.

Darren strapped it on and strummed it a couple of times. Examined the decal. "Blue Thunder," he said. "That don't even make sense."

"We can take it off," said Jon D.

"I don't want to take it off," I said.

"Look," said Jon D. "Darren's got a kit he's wants to sell."

"So," I said.

"So, maybe he'll trade it."

"Yeah," said Darren. "I'll trade it."

"No," I said.

"He'd rather play guitar," said Jon D.

"But I got the guitar," I said.

"Valvoline doesn't need two guitarists," said Jon D.

"What are you going to play?" I said.

"I'm the singer," he said.

"What if I won't play drums?" I said.

"That'd be too bad," said Darren. He pretended to windmill my guitar.

"His brother's place is next to a strip club," said Jon D. "Says the girls come over and do coke with the bands sometimes."

"I saw a stripper fuck a drummer's face once, backstage."

I shook my head, stared at both of them.

"So," they said.

"Jesus Christ," I said.

I told Mom the bad news, next morning at breakfast.

"Oh," she said. "Oh." She looked like she was in pain. Like someone had just punched her uterus or something. Mom didn't say another word. She stood up from the table and walked out of the kitchen. A piece of tape from work was stuck on the sole of her shoe. It made a slight tearing sound with each step she took away from the table. The noise made me want to cry for some reason.

Darren brought my drums over a couple days later. It was a cheap looking set with duct tape over a tear on the snare. I never learned to play them. Hard as I tried, I couldn't get my feet to synch up with my hands. At least that's what I told Mom and Dad. But honestly, I hardly tried at all. I'd just rhythmlessly beat the shit out of them when I got bored watching TV. And I could watch TV a very long time before I got bored. The band never performed in Ft. Wayne at a club next to a strip joint, or anywhere else for that matter. The closest we ever came to playing for an audience was when Steve signed us up for the Cromwell Community Center talent show, which we all attended just to hear an MC announce our names.

Mom never made it to Florida, either. But she did get a nice postcard from Cindy Kyle. On it was a picture of Snow White and the Seven Dwarfs at Disney World. All of them stood with perfect smiles on grass as green and manicured as a professional golf course. In the distance was water, impossibly blue. Same color as the cloudless sky over all their heads. On the back of the postcard Cindy wrote:

Dear Katherine,

Found your letters to Duke. Please don't send anymore. He's my husband, you dumb bitch.

Cindy

Joel was the one that found it in the mail. He gave it to Dad right away. Dad didn't get too upset when he read it though. I think it made him feel better. His dream had always been to find a good excuse to do nothing. Mom's affair had finally given it to him.

Eventually our elm died and rotted down in the front lawn. But before it did, Mom made a last ditch effort to save it. Put all her worth into healing the dumb tree. Skipped breakfast to water its withered yellow trunk and shriveled leaves. Ordered special dirt from a nursery. Even put compost around it. But it was already sick at the roots and everybody knew it didn't stand a chance.

One Day

Harvey Shapiro

Some lonely bird's insistence
that the sun rise.

The way mankind believes in a golden age
he believes in a time he had talent.

Thunder says the storm is approaching.
The chairs sit on the deck, waiting for rain.

The umber nipples
of the women of Lucca.

A bird moves through space
as if it contained corridors.

Jays jab at the world.
Their blue is not happy.

Children love dinosaurs because
if dinosaurs existed, we would not.

In his dream he came to his dead friend
for help. His friend said, take my place.

OPEN CITY

His goal was obscurity
but he kept blundering into sense.

He had no way of knowing
these were his exit lines.

Night in the Hamptons

Harvey Shapiro

Across the table, he watches her stick
her tongue up the man's ass. It goes deeper
as the dinner progresses—You were so great
on Charlie Rose, she says—he thinks
soon she will follow her tongue, up and up,
and disappear. But it doesn't happen.
The man's wife is cooly blonde and oblivious.
It is night in the Hamptons, over chopsticks,
waiting for the imperial war to begin. He
notices she has almost stopped slurping.
Soon the surf and the stars can move in.

"You're maudlin and full of self-pity," he said. "You're magnificent." (Dermont, page 95)

Four Round Windows

Written by Rick Rofihe
Illustrated by Thomas Robertson

He finished building a kite for no one
and gave it to the wind

and walked alone
past houses being built

and houses being torn down
and then he walked where there were no houses

except for one with four round windows.

"Things must look different
through round windows,"

he thought as
he went up close

but every time he looked in
one of the round windows,
all he saw was a reflection of his eyes,
two more round windows.

She finished making a boat for no one
and gave it to the water

and walked alone
past houses being built

and houses being torn down
and then she walked where there were no houses

except for one with
four round windows.

"Things must look
different through
round windows,"
she thought as
she went up close

but every time she looked in
one of the round windows,

all she saw was a reflection of her eyes,
two more round windows.

They walked together.

They walked past
houses being built

and wondered
who would
live there.

They walked
past houses
being torn down

and wondered
why no one
wanted to live
there anymore.

They walked and walked, past house after house

and then they

walked where

there were

no houses

except for the one with four round windows.

They looked in the first round window

 and saw four
round windows.

They looked in the second round window

 and saw four
round windows.

They looked in the third round window

 and saw four
round windows.

They looked in the fourth round window

 and saw four
round windows.

Then they looked away
from the round windows
of the house

to the round windows
of themselves that
met and

blinked and dodged
and met again
and....

...and stayed.

Now he would build kites
for her and the wind

and she would make boats
for him and the water.

Kites
  in the wind....

Boats
  in the water....

Things must
  look different

through four
round windows.

Some part of her was speaking to some other part of her, deciding something without her permission. (Brown, page 1)